CROC ATTACK

BY BRIAN GATTO

SEVEREDPRESS

CROC ATTACK

Copyright © 2025 By Brian Gatto

WWW.SEVEREDPRESS.COM

All rights reserved. No part of this book may be
reproduced or transmitted in any form or by any
electronic or mechanical means, including
photocopying, recording or by any information and
retrieval system, without the written permission of
the publisher and author, except where permitted by law.
This novel is a work of fiction. Names, characters, places and
incidents are the product of the author's imagination, or are used
fictitiously. Any resemblance to actual events, locales or persons,
living or dead, is purely coincidental.

ISBN: 978-1-923165-99-1

CHAPTER ONE

She would attack.

That primal instinct that dwelled within was desperate to take over. As far as the animal could recall, back to when she was a mere hatchling, barely able to hunt, this particular force dwelled within. The adrenaline energized her. It would eventually reach its peak when she had her prey encompassed in her elongated jaws.

The success of a hunt was akin to her basking in the sun on a hot summer's day. The release of neurotransmitter dopamine chemicals were always a telltale sign of the pleasure she was experiencing. Sometimes, she'd sit on a beach with her prey lying limp in her jagged teeth. Those times were the best of both worlds.

As the years progressed, there was no need to stalk her prey for her monstrous girth helped her to cover a long distance fast. She always moved unnaturally fast. Everything about her exterior design was against nature. Born from a creature of normality, it was mankind's doing that changed her mother's offspring.

Most of the hatchlings had perished mere weeks after birth. Some didn't even make it out of the womb. She, along with a few others had survived through the plague that was life. Out of the four of them, one choked on his own pollution intake, the other became a victim to her larger siblings. The last two of their particular and unnatural kind, they mated. After that, she never saw the male again. That was several months ago.

Now, at nearly fifteen years of age, she would be considered full grown. However she never stopped growing. First she passed ten feet which was a decent size for her species. Then came twenty; a gargantuan of her kind. Thirty followed close after. She now rested at thirty-two feet.

Thirty-two feet of massive power, she was a force not to be reckoned with. On top of her agility, pregnancy, and size, she was also starving. Her last meal was a panther that got too close to the water. In these scenarios she used to use her stealth to capture prey. It would prove rather fruitless though given she couldn't go too far into the shallows. Her scaly body always managed to peek out of the surface followed by her oddly bright yellowed eyes. She had attacked the hapless animal and consumed it before it managed to let out a yelp.

That was three days ago.

Searching for her next meal, she stumbled upon something. It was rather crude but still managed to garner her interest. She pressed her bumpy snout against it when suddenly it shot to the surface. Thinking nothing of it, she began to descend. A lightweight object bopped her on the head and continued to sink.

Boom!

She would attack.

Richie Stillwell and Glen Porter sat aboard their flimsy boat. It was more so a bathtub with an engine but Glen didn't care. He liked living the roughneck Cajun lifestyle. Living off the land, taking whatever was necessary to survive. Richie on the other hand was a basic consumer. He took whatever he wanted without worrying about the repercussions.

Case and point, when Richie lowered their net into the water Glen made a statement about them having enough fish to last them the weekend. It seemed that Richie wouldn't listen at first but, much to Glen's surprise, he began to retract the net.

"That's a good lad," Glen said with a phony Scottish accent.

"I'm not much younger than you."

"Give yer self five more years and you'll feel as old as I." He wasn't giving it up.

Richie chuckled and then stopped dead in his tracks. His hand over hand motion to pull up the net ceased and he looked right into Glen's eyes.

"There's something 'n it, eh?" Glen continued his forced dialect.

"Will you quit it with that accent already?" Richie looked down at the water. ". . . and for your information, yes. I just felt something huge bump into it."

An eagerness that could only be described as foolish showed on his childish features as he pulled and pulled on the net. Glen suppressed a chuckle. There was no way something charged at that net. It was barely even useable and, to add on top of it all, there was no bait attached.

Unsurprised to find his assumption was correct, Glen threw back his head and howled as Richie pulled in an empty net. The man looked beside himself but Glen didn't really care. He reached for the engine. It was getting late and it'd be too dark to be out on the everglades soon; especially with their dull flashlight.

"Wait!" Richie exclaimed. "I know there was something on that net."

"Aye, quit it while yer ahead, Rich. Let's get back before it gets too dark ta do so."

"What, is Mr. Scotty too afraid he'll crash our boat? Maybe he'll not be able to reverse the polarity." Richie belly laughed and even Glen couldn't help but smirk at that one.

His hard face returned once Richie pulled out his lunchbox and withdrew a red stick. There were two of them. Each had a wire attached to an end. They were held together by duct tape.

"Don't you do it, boy."

"You don't scare me, old man." Richie took out his pocket lighter and, before Glen could say any more, he lit the fuse. "Eat this!"

Tossing the dynamite overboard was the worst thing Richie could've done for a number of reasons. One: It was illegal and two: it was suicide.

With the upcoming bubbles frothing on the surface, a pair of hideous jaws reached out and snapped onto Richie's dynamite-throwing arm. He was tugged into the water before Glen could even process what had happened.

Richie was gone, taken into the murky waters of the river. Glen's mouth turned into an O-shape but his words were stifled once he saw blood rushing to the surface. He slowly turned around, his whole frame shaking, as he struggled to pull the cord on the engine. Thankfully, the old tub started up right away.

Glen drove away as if nothing had happened. He was rigid with fear and was still the whole way back to his shack. He'd have no friend to share a bottle of whisky with tonight.

The crocodile had killed her first human. It was much easier than sneaking up on other kinds of prey; especially because this meaty being was already in the water – her domain.

Chomping down on the frail hand and snapping the bone before pulling the rest of the attached body with her down into the blackness was satisfying to say the least. She quickly performed a death roll underwater to soften her prey. It was more for showcase though. She had no need to have her prize bloat. Instead, the victorious maneuver would be seen by nothing. However, she felt all the glory. She basked in it and then swam out further. A blood cloud trailed behind from her mutilated meal.

She thought back to her mate - if only for a fleeting minute. Would he have rejoiced in her successful hunt as much as she? Instead of focusing on the what-ifs, her scale-ridden body swam outward. Soon, she found herself resting on the bottom.

Richie Stillwell's body wasn't devoured yet. It still hung out of the crocodile's mouth as she lay. Overtime, other scavengers like a snake, two turtles, and even a small bull shark feasted off morsels from the hovering corpse.

Those brave enough for a second bite found they were able to do so without threat. The crocodile had shared enough when all that was left was Richie's arm and part of his torso.

She opened her cavernous jaws and swallowed him whole. There would never be a trace of what killed Richie Stillwell. So many predators had feasted upon him. The largest chunk was swallowed. The teeth marks would throw off other hunters, pursuers of her.

It was as if he never existed.

CHAPTER TWO

The high school yearbook.

Such a leather-bound physical edition told stories. Happenings such as Todd Winslow making the captain's position of the football team, Rachel McCormick being voted prom queen, and Tanner Felton being bestowed the honor of the class president. All these achievements seemed to mean the world to them at the time they occurred. However, after high school, those events drifted away and made way for their futures.

The last Tanner Felton heard of Todd Winslow he was going pro until he broke his shoulder blade and couldn't play, therefore didn't make it to team captain. Tanner often thought of that hard blow he must have felt; like a punch to the stomach.

Rachel McCormick was a beautiful woman now. Tanner often kicked himself for not asking her out. She seemed interested but he was too preoccupied with his decision to pursue high school politics to take action.

Then there was Tanner himself. Nearing his mid-twenties, there was so much potential out there waiting for him. In his college days he had gotten involved with some eco-activist group who wanted to preserve nature.

This group however turned out to be radical in their approach and wanted to cause damage and harm to those thought to be ruining the environment. He got out of there in a jiffy. They were obviously mad and chastised him. Their leader even tried to get him kicked off the college campus he was at. Thankfully the dean wasn't on board with that.

Those were different times.

Regardless, Tanner didn't give up. He and his brother Kyle decided to form their own protect-the-earth organization. It was one that didn't involve the violence or even interactions with those who were thought to be doing wrong to the world.

Instead, they'd look for alternatives for things such as wasted plastic and gas guzzling. Over time though, both Tanner and Kyle stopped believing in global warming being the cause for all of society's future problems and decided to focus on animals.

Tagging and tracking became their aim in the game. They'd do this with sharks, whales, and even some endangered reptiles. Kyle had brought in an old time friend, Dallas Jacobson who could help them with money issues.

Kyle had explained to him that their funding was running out because their financers weren't interested in friendly activists. Tanner suspected they wanted a television gig out of the whole thing.

Dallas was reluctant at first. He had a nice life in Arizona and two great sons. However, after their mom died, he wanted to get out and travel. His eldest, who was twenty-two at the time, decided to take his sibling and go to visit their aunt in Pennsylvania.

Dallas appreciated this and said he'd be back with all kinds of souvenirs. On long trips he'd call them to check in. Lola Besser admired him for his commitment to his family. She was from Australia and knew that family should be cherished. She also had a bit of a crush on the cowboy.

Mitch Carter was a bit of a pain in the ass, especially to Lola. It wasn't that he was a bad guy. He just didn't know any better way to get people's attention. Everyone could see this except Mitch himself and Tiffany Baker.

Baker had been hitting on Mitch since the first day they arrived at the Florida everglades. She was brought in as a student along with Mitch who both needed this class for their majors. Lola was an exchange student and wanted to see what it was like not to hunt animals but protect them. At least like in America.

The six of them made the team, the *Hissstory Makers*, out to be a pretty solid bunch. Tanner was very pleased with everyone's initiative and dedication. Even if some of them, like Tiffany, really didn't want to be there. Regardless, they managed to do their work and not complain.

They did have trouble showing up on time though.

By the time Dallas pulled into the driveway of the apartment complex Tanner and Kyle were staying at, the brothers had finished loading all their stuff into the van. The items included the basic home away from home supplies as well as camping gear.

As Dallas parked his truck into the driveway, Kyle noticed the pair of bull horns on the grill. He chuckled, as did Tanner, who almost didn't because he thought it looked awesome. The truck door opened and a pair of cowboy boots hit the ground with a *clack*. From there, dark blue denim jeans and a white button down shirt came into view. Soon, the hard face of Dallas Jacobson became clear and he walked over to the two men.

"Any room for my stuff in there?" His voice was deep. Kyle often wondered if he'd be any good as a country singer.

"We already got our gear in there so there should be plenty," Tanner stated in that official tone he used to give a sense of authority.

Dallas took out his camping gear and another small bag for his bathroom supplies and heaved them into the van. He then made his way around to the side of the vehicle and smirked. It was lime green and looked like something straight out of the 60s.

"Where on earth did you get this contraption?"

"From our uncle," Kyle began. "When his wife died he handed it down to us. He said there was no need to travel anymore without her so he thought we could make good use of it."

"It's got a nice paint job, that's for sure," Dallas said with a nod towards the shaggy ride.

"Did you get ahold of the others?" Tanner asked Dallas with that same authoritarian voice.

"Yeah, Lola is driving down with Tiffany, and Mitch was hitching a ride with… someone. He wasn't quite clear."

As if on cue, a loud hiss was heard. It was an expulsion of gas from the exhaust on a huge truck. The three men's heads turned and saw the cargo bed was massive. Then they saw the front of the vehicle. There was a grizzled driver and a fresh, young face in the passenger's seat.

When his hulking transportation came to a stop, Mitch Carter hopped out of it and ran over to the three men who were staring up at the eighteen-wheeler. Perplexed yet intrigued, they watched as it drove on and then disappeared down the street.

"Your friend seemed to be in a rush to leave," Tanner said to Mitch as he stopped running and began to trot over.

"Who, him? I don't know much about him so I wouldn't really call him a friend," Mitch chuckled.

Coming to a full stop, Mitch looked at them and their somewhat annoyed features plastered on their faces; especially Tanner's. "What..?"

"You hitchhiked?" Tanner asked more so than stated.

"Yeah, so? I wasn't going to have one of you travel all the way to Washington to come pick me up."

"You do realize it's illegal to hitchhike, right?" Kyle questioned the man.

"Wha... really? I never knew that." Mitch smirked ever so slightly.

"Idiot," Dallas mumbled.

Mitch paid the cowboy no mind and, instead, brought his stuff over to the van. He loaded it in and then turned to face the others. "So... where are the girls?" he said with a sly look.

"Let's keep this professional," Tanner said to the eager man before him. "I don't want any complaints of harassment."

"I, sir, am a gentleman at heart. You don't have to worry about me." Mitch gave him a half-hearted salute.

As if on cue, a red convertible drove down the street. Drove was putting it lightly. Tiffany Baker had the car going at fifty on a twenty mile per-hour street. Soon, the tires screeched and the vehicle came to a much needed stop.

Lola Besser got out first and stretched her muscular figure. She stood five-seven at least, had blonde hair, and a shiny white smile that was visible when she yawned.

Tiffany got out and chuckled at her. "This crazy bitch slept through most of my stunts."

Bringing her hands down to her sides quickly, she smiled. "You call those stunts?"

To Tanner, it seemed the snappy exchange between the two didn't seem angry or personal. They were just kidding around and he was thankful for that.

Mitch was taken aback by Tiffany. The woman was five-four, had shiny dirty-blonde hair, big brown eyes, and a buxom chest. She was easier to get to know than Lola in his mind. Lola was obviously out of his league.

He had met Tiffany once before during a video chat for a debriefing between the six of them. Her camera was off. He rushed over to help her with their bags.

After the gear was loaded and everyone piled into the tight quarters, Tanner put the key in the ignition and, to his surprise, it started up right away. He was fully expecting an irritating sound to come once he turned the keys – he wasn't too familiar with cars. There had been some problems with it and tuning it up never seemed to help. The last visit must have done the trick.

"Everybody ready?!" he asked excitedly.

Everyone cheered in unison and the six co-workers drove out of the parking garage. The apartment Tanner and Kyle were staying in was two blocks away from the garage so it was nice to finally be leaving that pit behind.

It wasn't a terrible room they stayed in but it could've been much better. Still, the trip from Miami, Florida to Graceville and then to the everglades wouldn't be more than forty minutes and it'd give them time to scope out a new apartment to stay in.

Kyle forgot to tell Tanner that he hadn't booked anywhere until this particular morning. Tanner had spent a better part of the early hours of the day searching through. There were a couple of openings. One was right on the everglades in fact.

Tanner told Kyle to consider himself lucky.

***

The curtains were closed but light still peeked past them and into her room. Emma Darwin rubbed her eyes and gave a light yawn. She rolled over on her queen-sized bed and put her arm around a pillow. Hugging it closely, she gave herself a few minutes to wake up.

Time ticked by and her position stayed the same. Eventually, she managed to get out of bed and over towards her bathroom. She gave a glance back over at her bed. It looked so inviting. However, she had work to do.

She flicked on the bathroom light and started up the shower. She looked in the mirror and saw her beautiful features.

Her naturally bright red hair went a bit below her shoulders and wasn't frizzy or messy. Instead, it was wavy and looked like it didn't even need to be done up. Her piercing dark brown eyes then gave her a once over. She was a busty, fit bird for being forty years old.

Stepping out of the shower fifteen minutes later she began to get ready for the day. After dressing and applying the essentials: make-up, extra hair products, and eyeliner, she walked out into the hallway.

A chandelier hung in the center of the pathway. She always admired it on her way out. It reminded her of her parent's old home. Her mother always loved them too. She'd bring a new one home after she returned from her business trips even if there wasn't room to fit one. God rest her soul.

Stepping down the stairwell, her chauffeur waited for her. He took her briefcase that she had packed the night before and, together, they made their way outside and towards the limousine.

As the elongated black car drove down the familiar back roads of the Floridian city of Graceville, the overhanging palm trees created reflections on the outside of it. Emma took the time to appreciate the meticulous precision of having each tree planted exactly six-feet apart. The strip went on for at least a mile and was always the highlight of her mornings.

Her chauffeur looked into the rearview mirror and smiled. Even though she was twenty years older than him, he appreciated her admiration for the little things in life. Most political figures he drove around didn't even look up from their phones.

It was as if she read his mind and looked at her phone. However, it was for a reasonable purpose. She was receiving a phone call.

"Hello, Ms. Darwin speaking."

"Hello to you, Emma," a gruff voice replied.

"Hey, Dad," Emma smiled and returned to looking out the window as she spoke. "What's up?"

"I think we ought to discuss the upcoming election a bit more."

"What about it?" Emma asked.

"Well, I just think you need to be a bit more conscious of the exterminators and hunters in the area."

Emma sighed. "I'm pretty lenient with their permits, Dad."

"Yes but they are having trouble getting any good game, given all this activist crap."

"Yeah well, they are pretty persistent in doing what they love."

"Oh please, you don't honestly support those hipsters?"

"No, I don't support the hipsters, Dad. I just support animal rights. Now, that's not to say that we can't hunt them but driving any species to extinction is never a good thing."

"Priorities, Emma. That's what makes for a successful career. Prioritizing the most important things first and then focusing on extra stuff secondary," Gregory Darwin explained as his daughter mouthed his words.

She had heard all this before and used it to get successful in her own right. Still, her father insisted on always reminding her. It wasn't a bad philosophy and she always gave it a second thought. She ended up settling on the fact that it never hurts to be told again.

"Alright, I'll have a meeting with them tomorrow or something. Today, I've got to meet some people and discuss the next election with the sheriff." She immediately slapped herself on the forehead because of her latter statement.

"Why are you talking to him about it instead of with me?"

"I just need a second opinion on a few things."

"I'm sure whatever you have to discuss with him can be talked about with me and be resolved quicker."

"I'm sure of it, Dad. I'll call you later; we're just pulling into the parking lot now."

They were still ten minutes away from the office.

"Okay, Emma. I expect to hear from you before dinner tonight," he said with great emphasis on his request.

"Yes, Dad, I'll keep in touch."

He hung up without saying goodbye.

The palm tree pathway that led to Graceville's city hall entrance reminded Emma of the trip to said building. Its sand-white pavement was inviting to say the least. The limousine pulled into the parking lot and her chauffeur got out. Opening the back passenger door, Emma was greeted with the warm salty air. It wasn't unusually windy and the light breeze made her hair fluff out a bit. It was a natural-made hair dryer.

Her chauffeur escorted her to the parking lot exit that led to the building itself. However, the sheriff was standing between the gaps. He raised his arm and ushered Emma to follow him. She did so and waved her chauffeur goodbye. He didn't question what was wrong for he not only trusted the sheriff but knew it wasn't his place.

"What's going on, Eugene?" Emma asked the sheriff.

There was a pause followed by a disappointed look on his face. "The hunters are waiting outside for you."

"What do they want?"

"They want a lot of things. Free range hunting, no limitations of guns, real wives, not mail-ordered ones and such. Except right now they want to talk to you about our incoming guests."

"I sort of guessed that," Emma said as she and the sheriff approached the crowd of at least fifteen men.

"Mayor, we need to talk!" A rather large hunter approached the two first.

"Yes, we do. However I will schedule a meeting for as early as tomorrow to discuss our visitors."

"Tomorrow will be too late. They'll already be here!" Oliver Jones, the only reasonable one of the bunch, spoke up.

Emma sighed. "I will talk with you and a few others of your party in my office in two hours. Meet me in there. We'll discuss a few things and you can relay the information to these gentlemen."

"Why not just tell us now?" the larger hunter shouted.

A bunch of agreements were spoken in loud, angry tones in unison.

"Alright, everybody calm down!" the sheriff spoke up.

There was a silence over the people. Emma was impressed and taken aback by his booming voice. He must be getting fed up with all this hoopla too.

"I need to go over a few things before anything can be said." She hoped they would buy that.

"Just tell us what's going to be done. What regulations are going to be put in place?" Oliver asked as politely as he could.

Emma buckled. "We've already informed a one Tanner Felton to not let him or his team interfere with your hunting. He said that there will be no problem and they're there to tag, not instigate," Emma said.

They all seemed somewhat satisfied. Enough so that they began to walk away.

CHAPTER THREE

It was a bad year.

With time to kill, Glen Porter sat at his favorite stop, Gills 'n' Grill. It was a shanty little bar and restaurant held up by a poor structure made of rotted patches of wood in places and cement filling in others. They served warm beer and crappy sea food. At least the service was nice. Beyond that though the only other reason Glen liked to be there was because it was his first job.

He used to make a mean lobster roll and had it served by the plateful for eagerly paying customers. Tourists and even regulars frequented Gills 'n' Grill back then however it wasn't called that. Originally it was called Sea Stuffer. Glen often chuckled to himself and wondered where people got these names from. Regardless of names, Sea Stuffer was bought out by a random man who paid very little for it.

Apparently the original owner, his boss, owed a lot of money to someone and this was his only way out. He never heard from his employer again. However, Glen didn't leave like everyone else. He called it integrity and they called it obsession. Things went south when he was fired for his tardiness. He didn't have a car back then. Still didn't. It made it a chore to get anywhere on time.

He moved on to working at a sawmill. It was planned to be close to the water to trim down floating logs that could get clogged where the river reached its peaks. Little coves were always drying up because the beavers would use the twigs and branches to make their homes. The sawmill was a way to fix it. It did its job until it was flooded a few years into the operation.

From there things went downhill fast. Glen was jobless and began to live and cook on his boat. Still, he couldn't bring himself to stop going there. He never understood why he kept coming through its door.

The beer was bad, everything was overpriced, and the food was atrocious. It was now being cooked by some self-indulgent yuppie by the name of Sergio. *Well Sergi-go, ya schmuck.* Glen often would think that to himself and get a little rise out of it. God knew the beer never would.

Still, the service was nice.

A petite little brunette by the name of Mary would serve the lukewarm drinks with a smile. She wasn't buxom enough to leech off a big businessman nor was she pretty enough to be a model. Still, that smile always warmed his heart. She couldn't have been older than nineteen.

Then there was Juanita; or as everyone called her, Juanita ta. She had slept with a lot of the patrons and even a few tourists. Thankfully, she wasn't hard on the eyes with her dark eyes and even darker hair. Still, she had a reputation that most knew about.

Tonight Juanita had her eyes set on a man in a suit who had his face in his bottle. Glen felt bad for the guy. He probably just got terminated from his job or lost out on some big promotion if Glen were to guess.

Tempted to warn the guy about Juanita, Glen was about to get up but Juanita saw this and strutted forward. He sat back down.

The tiger was on the prowl.

"Hi there," Juanita said in a peppy voice.

"Hello there yourself, toots," the suited man slurred.

"May I be blunt?" she asked sternly.

The man waved his hand for her to say what she had on her mind. "Go for it."

"It's just that… you're dressed awfully fancy to be in a shithole like this." She whispered the *shithole* part.

"I was supposed to be dressed fancy elsewhere with my wife tonight."

"Oh?" Her face beamed.

Maybe the guy had relationship issues or was in the middle of a divorce. She wasn't sure. Either way worked for her though. However, she'd gladly take the latter. It was best not to get mixed in with an affair.

"Yeah, I just got back from the hospital. Turns out, walking down the street with a nice tux can get you more than laid."

"What do you mean?"

"Sugar, I was robbed tonight. My wife was taken away from me along with three dollars and change."

For the first time in a long time, Juanita felt something. There was sorrow in her tone when she spoke next. "Want some company?"

The man gave a slightly irritated sigh and then pushed out the chair next to him.

She sat in the chair slowly.

Glen was shocked himself. The third idea he had for the guy was that it was all a sham and he was a dumpster diver. He called the kinds of people who looked for company dumpster divers around here. Mainly because people like him who came to this area were looking for trash.

After hearing his short yet sad story that was being told to Juanita, he told the bartender to fill his flask. He then walked outside to give the two a bit of privacy.

***

The sign read *officers parking only* but no one seemed to care. It was a laidback community and Sheriff Eugene Winslow knew that going in. Everyone liked the way things were. So when he got transferred and had those sign posts installed, no one batted an eye. To them he was just another officer of the law who liked to put up signs.

He was getting sick of it.

Today especially when he saw Martha parked in his usual spot. He drove around and, after getting cut off by an eager parker, he managed to find a spot. It was a good hundred feet from the door but at least his patrol car was here and he was on time.

Opening the door, a small car drove right towards him. He quickly shut the driver's side door and had to take a few seconds to breathe. Then, a small man got out of the car. He had a short-cut beard and glasses as well as a coffee mug that read *Jamin' Joe* on the side. Eugene was familiar with the hot spot that was *Jamin' Joe* and knew exactly what this kid's priorities in life were.

Fuckin' hipsters.

Sheriff Eugene Winslow opened his door and tried to shimmy his way out of the car. He almost nudged into the puny vehicle next to him and stopped to catch his breath.

"Please don't hit my car."

He looked up and saw the little twerp standing there staring at him. "What, like you almost hit mine?"

"Whatever, just be careful. I got a new paint job on there," he said but didn't leave.

It was obvious this guy wanted to make sure his little bug wouldn't be harmed. The sheriff figured he'd have the state pay for it. This irked Eugene and, on top of it all, the hipster had a whiny voice.

Finally, he got out of his truck. It took twice as long as it should have. Mainly it was because of the turd staring at him. He wasn't threatening in the slightest but his insistence on being careful and his persistent brown eyes looking at him didn't help the sheriff's blood pressure.

Then, there it was, a scraping sound. Sheriff Eugene Winslow looked and saw that his truck had scraped the bug. He figured that his weight lifting off of the truck positioned it in a way that was closer to the guy's car. *Ah shit.*

Looking back at the guy, more scared than he intended, he was surprised to see that he wasn't fuming. Rather, he had a calm look to him and he walked statically towards him. He wore an expression that said he was either inwardly pissed or holding back a fart. The sheriff couldn't decide. "I'll be billing the state."

"Okay." The sheriff remained calm. "I'll be expecting your call."

"I'll be emailing you, Sheriff. No need to hang up the busy phone line, am I right?" He gave the air a nudge as if he were doing it to the sheriff.

Smart little prick, the sheriff thought. *If he actually nudged me I'd arrest him right here and now. He probably knew that too.*

The guy then walked away. However, he wasn't heading for the police station. He instead turned and began making his way towards the news station. *He's a fucking reporter! No wonder he has a beef with me.* This aggravated the sheriff even though he wasn't all that surprised.

Graceville's local news was as honest as the big league news stations. Their opinions were biased and they hardly ever spewed facts. Instead, they twisted the words of the people and their elected officials. They preyed upon human emotion and played up angles that would otherwise be mundane.

A short time ago they were complaining about how Emma was pro nature yet the littering problem in Florida was, in simple terms, horrible.

The gullible ate it up.

Finally, Sheriff Eugene Winslow made his way towards the police station. He walked inside the front doors and saw his deputy nursing a cup of coffee and rubbing his temples.

"Frank!" Eugene shouted, his voice echoing through the spacious room.

Deputy Frank Gaston was always testing Sheriff Eugene Winslow on his patience. He particularly liked to torment him with false illnesses. Last week he had a migraine, this week he already had a stomach ache. However, today was for real. "Sorry Sheriff. I had a long night."

"Yeah, I can see that," Sheriff Eugene Winslow said as he stared into Frank's red-rimmed eyes.

"Won't happen again," Deputy Frank Gaston said. "Honest."

"Somehow, I don't believe you." The sheriff decided to pour himself a cup. "Anything interesting happen this morning, Becky?" He turned to the receptionist.

"Not much, Sheriff. Well, except for that exchange you had with Dean outside."

"Dean, ha! What a perfect name for such a tool." The sheriff laughed and then headed for his office.

***

The everglades surrounded them. Having acquired a fan boat, Kyle drove it with proficiency and grace. His five passengers had barely swayed as he made sharp turns in a wide sweep. Even Lola, the last person to be amused, was impressed. She along with the others gave cheers after every sharp-angled turn. Tanner also acted out-of-character and cheered his brother on; showing great admiration for his skills. Dallas was familiar with the maneuvering. His bull-riding days taught him the ways of body movement and how to correctly go with the flow. Tiffany had constantly raised her hands and screamed with delight. She mostly did that when he sped up getting ready to make a turn. Mitch was the only one unenthusiastic about the whole thing. His face had turned green multiple times.

At first everyone was having a great time and didn't realize that Mitch was getting sea sick. That was until Lola caught a glimpse. She touched Tiffany's shoulder. "Look who's a little green around the gills!"

Tiffany didn't want to but couldn't suppress her laughter. Dallas chuckled at him too. However, when Mitch turned to him, he appeared to be too focused to tease him. *He must take his riding seriously.* Mitch wondered why but didn't have the stomach to ask; neither literally nor figuratively. He just wanted it to end.

After a few more minutes, Mitch couldn't take any more and leaned over the side. He upchucked his breakfast and spread it across the water as they went. Tiffany looked back and gave a cry of disgust while Lola patted him on the back. "Nice   one!" Mitch gave her the finger from over his shoulder.

The boat came to a slow as Kyle pulled back the throttle. Mitch turned to him, furious. "Oh, now you stop the boat!"

"Well, we're here." Kyle grinned at him and then looked forward.

Mitch was about to argue until he followed Kyle's gaze and saw something that turned his frown upside down.

It was mystical. On a small atoll that sat in the center of a body of water, life seemed to stand still. The vibrant and lush greenery was inviting and felt like time didn't matter there. The first thing Mitch thought was that he never wanted to leave.

"I wonder what it looks like at night?" Tiffany asked no one in particular.

"Probably the same, just harder to see," Tanner continued to explain. "However, we'll be back in town way before dark."

"… But it's already twelve o' clock now!" Mitch said aloud.

"We'll be back bright and early tomorrow. Today, we're just scoping out the area," Tanner said.

Kyle brought the boat up to the shoreline where it brushed on the wet sand. It made a crunching sound that could be heard under the hull.

"Why's the sand like that?" Tiffany asked.

"It's an atoll," Tanner said.

"What does that mean?" she asked.

"You really need to pay attention in your classes, sweetheart," Dallas said in his deep cowboy twang.

Glaring at the Texan, she decided to remain quiet. Soon after, she returned her attention to Tanner.

He didn't wait for her to ask again. "That's the reason we're not spending the night here. Based on our calculations, by eight tonight, it'll all be underwater. The tide won't recede until seven or so the next morning."

"So, we'll be back by seven in the *morning*?!" she whined.

"Look, if you're not willing to get up at the crack of dawn like the rest of us, maybe you should just go home!" Kyle snapped.

"Easy, Kyle!" Mitch got between the two of them.

Tiffany admired that. While Kyle, on the other hand, began to get confrontational.

"I have planned this trip for you all," Kyle began. "It took me eight weeks to get the grants, approval from the school board, our rides including this one you love so much, as well as three hand-picked students and Dallas to come along. Now I don't expect gratitude but I do want people to pull up their bootstraps when it comes to getting their hands dirty, suffering some bug bites, and getting the hell up on time. Is that too much to ask?"

Mitch didn't back down right away. Instead, he turned towards Tiffany. "I'll grab your stuff."

Tiffany didn't say a word as he hefted her backpack along with his over his shoulder. He then hopped down and trudged up the sandy mound.

Kyle turned to Tiffany, held his hand forward, and smiled. "Ladies first."

She scoffed at him and saw Mitch holding his hand out for her. Taking it, she carefully hopped onto the atoll. As soon as she was settled in her place, she turned to Mitch. "Bugs?"

Mitch chuckled at that. He then wrapped his arm around her shoulder and ushered her over to the top of the central island.

***

It took half an hour too long to set up the equipment as far as Tanner was concerned. By the time they were settled in, it was almost quarter to four. He bit his tongue though. Kyle had already stirred things up enough with Tiffany and Mitch. No need to make the pot broil any further.

Lola and Tiffany were by a tide pool collecting samples and seemingly getting along swimmingly. Tanner wasn't sure if they would given their completely opposite personalities. Still, the occasional giggle brought warmth to his heart. He then turned over to see Mitch and Dallas getting nets ready. They had settled on larger holed netting that would catch bigger fish. Dallas was a pro at tossing it. It appeared like he was lassoing a noose whenever he threw it. Mitch stood by in the shallows with muck boots.

He turned to Kyle who was scoping out the area with high-tech binoculars. They had thermal and night vision functions that his brother eagerly wanted to try out; maybe not so much on this trip but the next one perhaps.

"Look over there!" Kyle said to his brother quietly as he passed him the binoculars.

Tanner followed Kyle's hand and then took them from him. "What is it?"

He raised them to his eyes and then saw that Kyle had had the night vision setting on. Through the device he saw Kyle's hand as it glowed orange. "Why do you have them on this setting?" "Because the sun's in the opposite direction and there's enough shade to not damage your eyes," Kyle explained.

Tanner had to admit to himself that there was no strain on his eyes and decided to follow his sibling's gesture. There was a lot of brown foliage that showed up as well as small creatures scurrying about, insects were flying around and Tanner could almost hear them buzzing in his ear. Then he saw it... or rather *them.*

There were three oval-shaped objects sitting in a small circular pit. It was obviously dug out. There were some brown spots on them having been caked in mud. It was hard to tell for it was caked on there and probably dried up. Tanner pictured himself picking them up and blowing the crust off them.

"Eggs."

"Not just any eggs. Big fuckin' eggs," Kyle chuckled.

Enamored by the sight, he then heard a huge splash. Quickly tearing his gaze away from the binoculars, he saw that Mitch and Dallas had something in their net.

The girls turned in time to see a scaly figure writhing around between the two men. Dallas wasted no time and, at the opportune moment, seized the reptile in a bear hug. It began to spin and spin as the cowboy held on for dear life. He managed to inch himself closer to shore as it wore itself out.

Jaws snapping, Dallas managed to wrap his hands around the reptile's mouth without losing any fingers. Lola was impressed.

"Tag it, tag it!" Dallas said quickly while exerting himself.

Kyle presented a small kit to Tanner who opened it, withdrew a syringe of some kind and slowly approached man and beast. Time seemed to slow as he made his way over.

Tiffany was static with shock. She kept repeating the same word. "Lizard!"

Tanner leaned over and stuck the needle behind the animal's ear. Or at least, that's where Tiffany suspected it was. He then pushed and a liquid shot into it. The great big reptile barely moved. Tanner backed off and then looked at Dallas. He nodded to the man.

Shooting up, Dallas backed off and let the creature go. It hissed at them and then slowly crawled back into the water. Mitch made his way out as it swam away.

"Lizard!" Tiffany shouted.

Everyone turned to her and chuckled.

"Try alligator, sweetheart." Dallas smiled.

"Stop calling me that!" she managed to snap back.

Dallas held up his hands in defeat.

Kyle turned to Tanner who was watching the last of the ripples fade in the murky water. He then returned his attention to his brother.

"I guess we know who made those eggs then," Kyle said.

"He was a male," Tanner said.

"Pretty big for an average alligator too," Kyle began to ponder. "Maybe Mama's around somewhere. Hell maybe they ain't even alligator eggs. For all we know they came from a chicken." He laughed.

Tanner didn't share his brother's enthusiasm.

***

It had been a long morning and an even longer afternoon. By nightfall Samuel Powers and Juanita were plastered. They had danced under the loose hanging disco ball and ate their terrible food and drank their warm beer. Eventually, Juanita leaned in for a kiss which was something she never did for her clients. To her surprise, Samuel accepted it. The man who just lost his wife was falling for another woman. Hell, Juanita couldn't believe she was falling for a man at all.

They were now walking hand in hand down the beach. Her curly dark brown hair blew and his tie whipped around in the aggressive wind. It didn't faze them in the slightest. Instead, Juanita grabbed him and planted a kiss on his rosy cheeks.

He smiled at her. "What was that for?"

"Come on, let's go back to my place."

It then dawned on him how far this was going. A sense of betrayal washed over him. How could he be doing this so soon after his wife's murder? So unbelievably soon that he counted it as cheating.

But there she was, Juanita with her great big smile and brown eyes, ushering him closer. Her small cleavage barely pressed against his chest. Still, she felt and smelled nice.

She talked nice too. At the bar she said all the right things on top of making all the right gestures. Samuel wasn't sure if she was a hooker but at this point he didn't care. No, she couldn't be. What kind of hooker actually cared about their client's feelings?

"Let's go for a swim." Juanita grinned.

He twirled her around like a ballerina and took her in. She was so pretty. It wasn't until she began to take off her purple dress with pink flowers on it that he began to become aroused. He had been admiring her without thinking of sex this whole time.

She is a special kind of woman, Samuel thought as he undid his annoying tie.

***

After feeding on a tiny predator that had dared to enter her cove, she swam up the canal in search of nourishment. The creature from the prior hunt was similar in appearance and texture but wasn't enough to curb her horrendous appetite. At her home there were signs of intruders beyond the morsel though.

Her senses picked up the smell of body odor that belonged to humans. It couldn't be distinguished as anything else for they had a distinct scent to them. From what she could decipher, there were at least five of them, maybe six. Two of which were in her waters.

Having overcome her rage on the intruders, a strange sense overcame her. For some curious reason, she wondered about the security of her eggs. Before she left she crawled ashore. Her massive girth glided on the muddy banks as she discovered upon further inspection that they were all undamaged.

Satisfied, she swam out of the cove and further into the everglades. Eventually, the shoreline appeared before her. It was lit up by luminescent orbs that hung from a line on sticks. The moon danced on the water and shone on the white sand making two targets become visible to the naked eye.

She needed no light however.

Sensing their presence by way of muffled sounds and smell, she was already over a quarter of a mile out and closing. The closer they got the more she slowed. If they were scared away it'd be a lost cause and she'd have to search elsewhere for food.

Coming to a stop, she soon sank to the bottom. The world above her turned into water and the ripples she caused eventually faded away. Everything returned to calm on the glassy surface. Below, she rested and waited for them to enter her domain.

***

Juanita was the first one in followed shortly after by Samuel Powers. At first they were walking in the lukewarm river but soon found themselves neck-deep. The water was pitch-black despite there being a full moon over the everglades.

Splashing him with delight, Juanita found that he was getting closer and closer to her. Soon, she took him in her hands and guided him into her. She moaned aloud and they kissed.

Embracing under the moonlight, they moved in rhythmic fashion causing the water to lap lightly. Her fingers dug into his back, her light pink nails ran across him carefully. However, they soon dug in and drew blood.

Before he could scream… she did.

Her cries turned into gurgles as a crimson substance spilled from her mouth. It took Samuel a second to realize that she was coughing up blood. She was soon dragged away and pulled under the surface.

"Juanita!" he shouted after her.

There was no response. Not even in the form of a bubble or a ripple. Soon, he found his legs were turning around and his arms working overtime to get him back to shore. His mind was still on the beautiful Latina whom he just had in his arms.

Working his arms like paddles, Samuel Powers was surprised how little time it took to get to shore. He crawled onto the white beach, the grainy sand causing him to chafe between his exposed legs. There, he began to cry.

Swoosh.

A sound that reminded him of pushing mud could be heard from behind. He didn't want to look but decided to regardless of what sat behind him on the beach. Slowly turning his head to look over his shoulder, a pair of hideous dark yellow orbs stared at him – eyes.

Soon, the massive maw of the crocodile opened and scooped Samuel Powers' lower half up, followed by slamming shut on his torso. It then pulled lightly and he came apart. The rest was left behind for the seagulls.

CHAPTER FOUR

There was no instantaneous cure.

Nursing his flask in his barely lucid state, Glen managed to pour some of the remaining bourbon down his gullet. He wasn't a coffee drinking man nor did he believe it cured hangovers. On this particular day however it seemed he'd need a miracle to snap himself out of it – a real kick in the balls.

Or a shocking sight.

As the sun poured through the glassless window frame, Glen Porter's shack glowed a yellow-orange hue. Dust particles danced around in the light. Dirt created a slight haze as he kicked it up from under his hammock. He swayed to and fro and finally he rose off the netted bed.

The sunshine made him squint. He thought of how that huge shining star during the day was supposed to be good for your skin. Chuckling, he dared another glance at it. It only seemed to bore down stronger upon him. It painted him in a godly image. "Healthy for the skin, my ass, more like cancerous," Glen maligned.

Both feet plated on the ground, he mustered through the shanty shack. Walking a few feet away from his hammock, he came into the kitchen and opened his mini fridge. There was nothing really edible in it, let alone tasty.

After what seemed like an eternity, he shut it and made his way back over to the window. Now that he was standing, the sun was at a different angle and therefore didn't hit his eyes. He could take in his favorite part of the day – the view.

Wet grass that'd suck your boots off and a running river that could sweep you away were what greeted him. It was a particularly dirty place besides the white sand beach.

His gaze turned to it and he noticed something strange. It wasn't a log but it did have a familiar mold to something he saw. It reminded him of a person but that couldn't be. It was way too short and round. Unless it was a midget sleeping off an all-night bender, he had to look for different possibilities.

Eventually he figured that the only way he'd find out is if he went to investigate. He turned his back to the window and made his way past the kitchen. Heading into the so-called den (which was really more an old weathered leather chair and a fire pit dug into the ground) he grabbed his hunting rifle from off the seat of the mangled recliner.

He then made his way outside.

There was no reason to take such a prolonged amount of time walking over towards this stump or whatever it was. Still, Glen had to be sure. As he approached, he caught a whiff of something fierce. He began dry heaving whatever was in his stomach – which wasn't much. Attempting to open his stinging eyes, the pungent odor made him tear up. Then he was staring wide-eyed. The pain seemed to disappear.

He had his answer.

***

Having just settled into his office chair, Sheriff Eugene Winslow was about to reach for his cup of coffee. The mug had been given to him by his receptionist whom he believed had been crushing on him. It had a picture of a police badge on it that had "Protect and Serve" written underneath. *At least she gets it,* Eugene smiled to himself. He had only just begun to think of that petty reporter from yesterday while reaching for his coffee when the phone on his desk rang.

Glen Porter was on the other end. He didn't have time to say the protocoled line of stating his name and asking how he could help. Instead, heavy labored breathing greeted him. He could tell it was Glen and could almost smell the alcohol on his breath through the phone as if he were somehow in the room with him.

"Body… near the water. It's awful, Sheriff!" Glen was trying to pace himself but just sounded short of air.

"Where are you, Glen?" Sheriff Eugene Winslow asked.

"Over by my home," Glen stated.

The sheriff thought of Glen's "home". It was more so a shack that barely had four walls to hold it up. It was a cesspool but the man seemed to make it fine while living there. He didn't even have a car; just that hand dandy rifle of his.

A thought crossed the sheriff's mind. Did he have something to do with the dead body? Eugene shook off that notion. Glen couldn't hurt anyone. He was good at killing gators but nothing that walked on two legs.

"Sheriff…?" Glen asked on the other end of the line.

"I'll be right there," Sheriff Eugene Winslow said gravely.

When the call was over, Glen couldn't help but feel that there was something off about the sheriff's tone. He didn't sound right; almost like he suspected him of something. The thought crossed his mind of being charged with being an accomplice to the crime or even committing the crime himself.

Right then and there he wanted to leave and never look back. However, he knew the sheriff pretty well and figured that he'd cover all angles before jumping to any conclusion. He would do fair observations before coming to a decision of any kind.

That nagging feeling stayed with him. Glen eventually decided to stay right where he was. Everything was going to be alright.

About twenty minutes later a truck pulled up towards the beach where Glen was standing. The old gator-hunter's heart sank. The large vehicle's driver's side door opened and a pair of muck boots could be seen stepping out one at a time.

Vince Warner was wearing sunglasses with his light brown hair slicked back. He was donning the fish and game outfit that was perfectly within regulations. The look he had was down pat to the perfect warden. However, besides being by-the-book, he was not the nicest guy.

Approaching Glen with a casual stride that still intimidated, he gave a faint smile that was barely noticeable given the harsh sunlight. Vince decided to go easy on Glen at first and then give him the low-down on what was going to happen. It was not every day a human body washed up on shore.

"Remind you of anything…?" Glen asked the fish and game warden who seemed a bit surprised that Glen didn't seem ready to submit to him just yet.

"What? You mean like your fishing partner?"

"Richie was a good man and an even better *hunter*." Glen's temper was showing.

"Yeah, well. Anyway, tell me what happened here," Vince asked.

"I was at a bar last night, saw this man with Juanita. This morning I see this man again however he's half eaten on the beach. I don't know if Juanita is alright or if she's somewhere out there." Glen gestured towards the water.

"Were there any signs of tension between the two?" Vince asked.

Glen was a bit surprised. Vince was actually investigating a probable gator attack. Usually he'd just get the police involved and sit at his desk back at headquarters. However, that surprise gave way for Vince to ask another question of semi-importance. "Did you talk to them?"

"What, no. I just left when they began to get too loud and frisky." Glen was still in control of himself.

"Interesting…" Vince smiled. "Did you see them go to the water?"

"No," Glen said, annoyed.

"Did you hear anything strange last night?"

"Nope. I was out like a light."

"Well alright. Let's have a look at this body."

"Shouldn't we wait for the coroner?" Glen suggested.

"I won't touch it, trust me," Vince said as he walked past Glen.

When Vince arrived, there was a slight smell. He chalked it up to being Glen's shack. However, after approaching the body, he discovered the odor's real source. He covered his mouth and nose with his arm and backed off. "That's ghastly!"

He turned around and faced Glen. After walking back towards the grizzled gator hunter he finally uncovered his mouth. He then looked up at him and saw that he was staring wide-eyed with horror.

There was a swooshing sound, like a rush of water. Vince turned around to see that the body was gone. All that was left were some red stains in the pearl white sand.

***

It could have been a lot worse given yesterday's deadly game of man versus reptile. After they let the alligator return to the water, Mitch had joked that maybe she'd come back and get Lola. She had a huge fit about that.

Kyle was still stuck on the possibility that those eggs that he and his brother saw through the infrared binoculars belonged to her. However, Tanner still had his doubts. They were much too large. It was a fact not lost on Kyle but he suggested that maybe pollution or even a bigger male alligator had something to do with it.

Dallas had put his feet up on the headrest behind Mitch and was playfully tapping his feet against his head, barely even touching the hairs on him. He had to suppress laughter that was building up from within him as Mitch kept trying to swat away what he thought was a mosquito.

Sitting next to Dallas, Tiffany was applying make-up. When she looked away from her compact mirror for two seconds however, even she tried not to giggle. The two of them were turning beet red.

Lola, who had reluctantly sat next to Mitch despite his jokey persona, turned and noticed this and smirked. Her facial expression changed when Mitch turned towards her.

"What?"

"Nothing," she said plainly and then returned to looking out the van's window.

By pure chance, Tanner looked into the rearview mirror. He saw what Dallas was doing and put a stop to it right there and then. "Knock it off, cowboy."

Dallas quickly placed his feet back onto the floor of the vehicle. "What's wrong?"

Mitch still didn't get it. He brushed the back of his head and decided to turn back. Dallas was just looking out the window while Tiffany made herself look sexy. When he turned back to facing the front, he figured that at least that annoying mosquito was gone.

Tanner looked down from the rearview mirror after the group in back settled down. He was refocusing on the road when he slammed on his brakes. Everyone lurched forward.

Ahead of the van, a deranged-looking man stood. He was wide-eyed with terror and looking around for something. Seemingly, the slightest brush movement would scare this man. It was as if he had seen a ghost.

Tanner took in his appearance. He was donning a tattered white shirt with a vest covered with pockets, a white fedora that had seen better days for it was tanned and dirty, and brown pants that probably covered up any accidents he might have had judging by his fearful mannerisms.

Quickly getting out of the van, Kyle and Tanner rushed to his aid. The rest of the gang stayed put. They decided inwardly that it'd be best for them to not get out unless needed. Dallas and Lola were at the ready but Mitch and Tiffany seemed hesitant.

"Are you okay, old timer?" Kyle asked the skittish man.

"She's back," he said while out of breath.

Tanner was surprised he answered right away. He thought that it'd be a challenge to get him to even mumble. Still, they had to keep probing him until they got a more cohesive answer. "Who's back?"

"I thought I left her in the bog." He was still being vague.

"What's going on? Who's she?" Kyle was getting worried.

Suddenly, the sound of sticks breaking and brush moving from afar could be heard. Both Kyle and Tanner froze in place. The old man was static, looking into the forest with them.

Back in the van, the gang was getting nervous. At first, Kyle and Tanner were just talking to the old guy. Now they were facing the forest as if something were coming for them. Lola fought against the act of reaching forward to honk the horn. It could scare whatever was out there off. Or, more than likely, it'd draw it towards them.

It was as if time stopped for Kyle and Tanner. Whatever it was that was out there, it couldn't be that big. Still, whatever scared this old man was now scaring them and, based on his expressions, it wasn't going to end well.

"Mr. Porter," a voice called from the woods. "Are you there?"

Glen didn't answer but instead just looked away as if the voice from the woods yielded no harm. Still, that left whatever else was out there that scared him ever so.

A man with a fish and game warden outfit appeared from behind the brush. He looked at the trio standing in front of the van and chuckled. "Ya'll look like you saw death."

"Maybe we did," Kyle insinuated.

Vince Warner didn't like the attitude the punk gave him but he let it slide for now. "What're ya'll doing here with ol' Glen?"

"He came out into the middle of the road, I almost hit him," Tanner explained.

"Okay." Vince turned to the grizzled gator hunter. "Glen, go home. I'll be by later to ask you further questions."

Glen could only nod slightly as he made his way past Vince and further into the brush.

"What happened to him? Why is he so spooked?" Kyle asked.

"Just a gator or sumthin'. He claims it got his friend a year back along with a couple of others..." Vince bit his tongue. He was always one to brag with his fellow fish and game buddies but tended to leak private information out to them as well. He had no idea why he just said what he did but he had to fix it somehow.

"Today?" Kyle was curious.

"Um, no. Around the same time."

"The same time as what?" Tanner began to question him too.

"As his friend."

"Somehow I don't believe that," Kyle pushed further.

"Why not?" Vince was beginning to feel small and he didn't like that.

"Because he's freaked out right now, something must have happened recently," Tanner explained.

"He's always like that. Look, you don't need to be here right now. Just go wherever you were planning to go and let's leave it at that." Vince's voice was rising.

Tanner and Kyle shrugged and then walked back to the van. Vince felt satisfied as they pulled away. He then made his way down through the forest and back to his truck. As he drove off, he noticed that the van was heading in the opposite direction it was before. Still, Vince had more pressing matters to attend to. He had got a call in about a gator, namely its severed head, showing up on someone's property and he had to remove it. Still, the dead body came first.

"He's going in the opposite direction," Dallas said from the back seat.

"Good, let's head back and see what happened over there." Tanner smiled.

"He's out of sight." Dallas grinned.

"… and so are we," Tanner chuckled.

Glen Porter sat in his tattered recliner. He pulled the lever and soon his feet were suspended in the air by a leather cushioning. He took a few deep breaths and pulled out his flask. The whisky poured down his throat and, for the first time in a very long time, he winced at the taste.

She was back and he was becoming sober enough to actually taste the alcoholic poison he'd be consuming day after day. He needed to snap out of it, be in control of himself. The crocodile needed to be stopped before she killed anyone else. Richie, Juanita, and some suit were dead. There was no time to ponder on who'd be next for a knocking sound could be heard coming from the door of his shack.

At first, he ignored the incessant sound. To him it sounded like someone pounding the rotted sheet of wood he called a door. In reality, Tanner had tried knocking carefully so the whole thing wouldn't collapse.

He knocked even lighter this time.

Whoever it was became a nuisance to Glen fast. The persistency of the person outside weighed on his patience. He could feel the vein on his temple pulsating and beads of sweat cascading down his oily skin. Finally, he slammed his feet down which made the whole chair shudder. He then got up and marched to the front of his barely standing home.

Opening the door, Glen was greeted by six young faces. Two handsome men, a scrawny kid, a cowboy, and two beautiful women stood before him. Their appearances didn't dissuade him from attempting to shut the door on their hopeful expressions.

Tanner quickly held his foot out and stopped it from closing. "We need to talk."

"Look, I don't know who you are or what you want. I do know that I ain't talkin' to nobody though. Now please move your fuckin' foot out of my doorway."

"Did you see the eggs in the swamp?" Tanner asked. He was grasping at straws to start a conversation, that much was apparent. Still, it was all he had.

Glen was taken aback. "What eggs?"

"Come on, Tanner. This old coot doesn't know anything." Kyle tried to usher his brother away from the grizzled man with one crazy eye and a veiny temple.

Tanner ignored his sibling and smiled. "You can't tell me that you hunt around here and that you didn't see those gator eggs."

Glen forced a half-hearted smile. "Gators are elusive. They also know that putting their eggs out in plain sight is a really dumb idea. No, I don't look for their eggs. In fact, I stop a lot of them from making 'em."

"So you're a gator hunter?" Lola asked with her voice raised.

"Lady, I've hunted snakes, big cats, and gators alike. They're all fair game." Glen was trying to poke the metaphorical stick at her but she wasn't backing down.

"You do know that there are other things to do than hunt big game for this particular region?" Lola asked.

He chuckled at that. "Big game, huh? So what'd you call small game around here then, ma'am?"

"Just go fishing, asshole." Lola's temper was rising.

"I would but then you and your people would complain when I'd go over the limit," Glen smiled when their expressions changed. "Oh yeah, I know all about you people. You're the nature activists who keep fucking with our nets while putting cherry bombs in our boats and trying to save animals by even more extreme measures than the two I just mentioned."

"Not really, sir." Tanner returned to the conversation. "In fact, we're on both sides. While yes we'd like there to be a limit on catch and game, we won't stoop to such drastic levels as tampering with people's supplies or livelihoods."

Glen scoffed at him. "So if you fight for both sides then who wins?"

"Nature," Tanner said matter of factly. "She can take care of herself but we're here just to lend a helping hand if need be."

"Mkay." Glen seemed a little less tense now but still remained slightly on-edge. "So, what do you people want from me?"

"We almost hit you with our van and just wanted to make sure that you're alright. Also, we were wondering why you looked absolutely petrified as if something was chasing you."

There was a drawn out pause between the activists and the hunter.

"Nuthin' was chasin' me. Just memories, that's all they were. Deadly reminders of the past, hauntings if you will, they were things I can't escape."

"What happened in your past, old timer?" Dallas asked.

"The name's Glen Porter and I used to not be such a recluse. I had a good friend, Richie Stillwell. He was eaten by a monstrous animal. A black bitch that was scale laden and smelled of the bog itself, she ate him and nearly me too," Glen continued. "I found a body on the beach this morning. Damn guy had been torn in two. The imprints in the sand were at least two and a half feet wide. That'd make this animal at least thirty feet long… maybe longer."

"What did it?" Tiffany asked with a shiver in her tone.

Glen paused for dramatic effect.

"Crocodile."

"A thirty-foot crocodile?" Mitch suppressed a chuckle.

"Go ahead, scoff at me. Be like the rest, non-believers. I thought she'd remain out there in the boggiest parts of the everglades. However, she's here now and soon, everyone will believe and no one will forget!"

CHAPTER FIVE

There was a lot to unpack.

As the group of six activists made their way into the city, Tanner kept pondering on the idea that the supposed gator eggs he'd seen had in fact belonged to a crocodile. Another thing that dug into his thoughts was the fact that if their mother was thirty-feet in length, would her offspring follow suit? Also, how'd she get so big? Was she a freak of nature, a result of chemical warfare, radiation? Now Tanner felt he was stepping too far into B-movie territory. Still, there needed to be a reason why something that big was around here.

The other possibility was that Mr. Glen Porter was just messing with them or even over-exaggerating. Maybe he wanted them to go poke around the river? Go far out and find nothing. Waste fuel and time, or even damper their hopes, it would all be a big joke to him. Glen had whisky on his breath. Maybe he was known for spewing tall tales of killer crocodiles and dead friends amongst his fellow bar patrons?

However, there was the angle that he was telling the truth that he kept coming back to. Tanner knew a couple of things for certain. The game warden was running after Glen, there was an unmistakable dark patch on the sand where the hunter had pointed that he didn't bring up, and there was a nest of oversized reptile eggs in that cove.

He kept reeling over everything as they made their way into the town. Graceville was a nice little city in Florida. Parts of it reminded him of a fishing village while others, a bustling New York street. It was quaint yet busy enough to keep the area packed with gift shops for tourists to enjoy and restaurants for their leisurely consumption.

The idea of restaurants made his stomach growl. "Hey, gang. Want to stop somewhere to eat?" he called over his shoulder.

"Sure!" everyone said practically in unison.

It wasn't long until they pulled into an appropriate appearing seafood restaurant. The name Gills 'n' Grill caught everyone's attention. That and the decent parking really made it seem inviting. Tanner pulled into a spot not too far from the building and the group walked towards the entrance.

Gills 'n' Grill on the outside was a red brick building with nothing too fancy in terms of designs. The most artsy it got was the two 'l's being in the shape of fish gills on each word. The logo was catchy and had a cool design. This was mostly noticed by Tiffany.

While Tiffany Baker was a vital part of the team, she was only doing this project for extra credit. She really wanted to be a graphic artist. On top of being skilled with hand drawings, her shining trait was computer art. She once told her parents of all the cool stuff they had in the classroom. They were most enamored by one particular device where you'd take a funny looking pen and draw on a tablet of sorts; it'd then show up on the computer at the same time. The Bakers were so impressed that they bought her a MAC and the pen to go with it for her last birthday.

Digital drawing became a passion of hers and, even as they sat down in this cozy restaurant, she felt the urge to doodle. She took in the interior and admired the white walls with red lights bouncing around. Their transparency wasn't fully clear and they created somewhat of a glow on the surrounding surfaces.

Mitch had watched Tiffany look around for the better part of twenty minutes now. She seemed to be mesmerized. It wasn't until she noticed him staring that she came back down to earth. Blushing, she gave him a smile.

Even though Mitch Carter wasn't built like Tanner or Kyle, nor strong like Dallas, she couldn't help but be attracted to him. He seemed like a decent enough guy and had a sense of humor to him that she found admirable.

He returned the smile and then faced the rest of the group. "He came from the deep!" he said in a faux ghostly voice. "Half man, half guts!"

Tanner wasn't impressed even though everyone else chuckled. Even Lola felt the tension lighten. The group hadn't really spoken about the half-eaten man Glen described.

"Sounds like we're having a good ol' time over here." Their waitress had arrived. "My name is Mary and I'll be serving you today."

Her pearl white smile dazzled Mitch right away. She was a buxom brunette who wore a red mini dress with white polka dots on it. Her hair had blonde highlights and had a wavy flow to it.

Tiffany didn't like this at all.

"What can I get ya'll for drinks?"

"I'll have water with lemon," Tiffany snapped at her.

Mary noticed but paid no mind.

The rest of the group ordered their drinks and mozzarella sticks for appetizers. A few minutes passed and the silence had returned. Not a word had been spoken between them.

Rather than break the tension with another joke, Mitch decided to say something he'd learn he shouldn't have. "She seems nice."

"Oh, I thought she was kind of snobby," Tiffany said while looking over the menu.

Mitch was not only at a loss for words, he seemed torn between two hot women. The blonde, petite city girl or the brunette country gal with the award winning smile, it was a tough call. Still, he was smart about it and stuck to what he was guaranteed. "Yeah, I didn't want to say anything but I thought so too."

Tanner and Kyle couldn't help but look at each other and snigger. Tiffany had Mitch wrapped around her little finger. The poor guy would probably never realize until it was too late.

There was a reason Tanner didn't ask her to become a permanent member of the team.

Meanwhile, Dallas and Lola were sitting next to each other in awkward silence. Their four peers all knew they'd make a perfect couple. However, they were the kind of people who needed the other person to make the first move.

Tanner had his bets on Lola while Kyle was hinging on Dallas to collect ten bucks. However, they'd both probably end up losing and neither the cowboy nor the Aussie would commit. Still, it'd be a nice surprise seeing as how Tanner wanted both of them on their next project.

After a few minutes, Mary came back with their drinks. She handed them out and said that their appetizers would be done soon. They needed more time with their menus so she promised to return in another few minutes.

"Ugh," Tiffany groaned in annoyance.

"What is it?" Mitch asked a bit too eagerly.

"The bitch forgot my lemon."

After eating their meals in silence, the group all chipped in to pay for the bill. When exiting the Gills 'n' Grill, Tanner was the first to speak. "Let's get to the boat."

"I'm stuffed," Mitch began. "Can't it wait until a bit later?"

"There's too much to do. Plus, if we wait even an hour it'll be dark before we leave."

"What'd you have in mind, Cap?" Dallas asked.

Tanner stopped and thought of about it. He had already laid out the agenda and already knew what the plan was. It was what Dallas called him. 'Cap' had a strong meaning behind it for him. He was their leader and in that he'd get them through their semester while still being wary of his title. He mentally shook the thought away. He was their captain, sure. However, he wasn't the kind of man to take advantage of people. That'd go against his principle.

"Well, we're going to go to the spot from yesterday but I want to scope around the outside of the cove."

"Why's that?" Lola asked.

"Because tales of giant crocodiles and seeing overly large eggs doesn't sit right with me and I just have to be sure," Tanner explained.

"Sure of what?" Mitch asked, somewhat annoyed. He sounded like he was trying to suppress a belch.

"That the waters around this area haven't been tampered with." He looked at the group who seemed confused. "Don't forget the test tubes."

Ten minutes later and they were at the docks. The sun was beaming on it. It shone so hard that the activists had to squint for most of their way down. They could make out that next to their boat was a familiar figure, however.

Glen Porter was looking less antsy than yesterday. He still donned the same white shirt, tan fedora, and brown pants from yesterday. Today, in the beating sun, his snow-white sideburns were ever prevalent. His face didn't hold any enthusiasm to see them, though. He still looked as grim as ever.

"What is it you want?" Tanner spoke up as they got within earshot of the man.

"Look, I didn't want to stoop down to this. Working with a bunch of tree huggers really isn't my style."

Tanner was getting annoyed with everyone assuming their occupation. "We're not tree huggers, damnit. We help as much as we can but at the end of the day we know that the earth can save itself. Things like untangling nets around porpoises, tagging animals to track, or preserving an endangered species are what we do."

Glen smirked. "Then you'd probably want to go under a different title than activist. That word there don't sit right with us hunters."

"Why'd you meet us at our fan boat then?" Kyle was getting annoyed and wanted to get out towards the cove as soon as possible.

There was a pause. It was long enough to make it seem like Glen had forgotten himself why he had come down there.

"I want to rent your boat."

Tanner looked down at the water. There was a little dinghy. It could barely hold one person it seemed, let alone two or three. He noticed that it didn't even have an engine. He then turned back to Glen who had noticed him observing his boat.

"It won't be big enough," Glen said.

"You want to hunt the animal that killed that man yesterday?" Mitch sounded like he was pleased with coming to that conclusion.

"No, I wanted to go for a leisure ride into the river and hopefully catch myself a baby anaconda; yes, ye feckin' idiot, I want to take her down."

Yesterday, Glen said that "she" was back. *Is she the one that killed that man and laid those eggs? Or was Glen just delusional?* Kyle couldn't tell but he was leaning more towards the latter. But then he thought of the tracks in the sand and his mental decision scale began to sway towards the former.

"What is she?" Tanner asked the question on everyone's mind.

"She's got to be forty feet at least. Damn creature. Her black scales covered in barnacles, yellow eyes like a cats-eyes, and that fuckin' maw that can stretch so wide and take my best friend away."

The group remained silent.

Finally, Tanner spoke. "We can't have you take our boat, I'm sorry."

Glen looked almost shocked.

"Come on, guys." Tanner ushered his friends onto the fan boat.

Glen watched as Tanner put the keys in the ignition, started her up, and drove off into the everglades. He was furious. "If you meet up with her you'll need more than test tubes and beakers to take her down!"

He knew they couldn't hear him but his rage was satisfied by that statement. It was true and those kids needed to be better prepared.

About two minutes into their journey, Lola pulled out the camera. She took some pictures of the wildlife in its natural state of serenity. There were a couple of fishermen they passed. One had waved his hand while the other his fist.

Tanner saw this and decided to ease up on the throttle. No need to scare everything so close to shore.

Soon, they were pushing fifteen miles per-hour at best. Lola was able to get better pictures now. She saw a seagull land on a piling on a dock. It leaned over to observe a plastic bag in the water. She thought it'd make a great photograph. The stillness would show a bird contemplating about the state of the environment before swooping in and taking the bag, no doubt to stop any other animal from doing the same. She shuddered at that angle. It sounded like she was for the opposing team. That team would take such a photo with the same tagline and then rush to blow-up a company that made plastic bags or something. They'd scream it was all for nature and they'd probably get away with it.

She raised her camera to take the picture anyway. She'd work with a different tagline. As she positioned the lens to focus mainly on both objects, a dark brown colored figure slid from the water and snatched the bird. It then returned with its prize as if it had never been there to begin with.

Lola fell back onto Mitch's lap. "Whoa, are you alright?!"

Taking a few deep breaths, she looked up at Mitch and then got up to sit back in her seat. "Yeah, it's nothing that I haven't seen in Australia tens of times."

It was true that Lola had seen that sort of thing happen often back home. However, she chalked up her gasping reaction to the fact that she was so immersed in trying to get a good picture that it caught her by surprise.

She sat back and leaned her head on the headrest as they drove on.

The alligator had its prize. Ripping into the soft, feathery skin, the flesh soon came apart. The water turned pink with sinew floating about. The reptile shook its prey to and fro until it was soft enough to swallow.

As for the seagull, like most animals, it never saw the predator coming. It didn't even have time to react. Death came quickly to the bird.

Now that the prey was tenderized, the alligator began to scoff it down. All of a sudden, the bird flew out of its mouth as well as a rush of blood. It felt its stomach collapse as well as it being dragged down into the murky depths.

Something much larger had killed the predator.

***

Sheriff Eugene Winslow entered the fish and game warden building with a stick up his butt from what Vince Warner assumed. Here he was, blabbing about how he should've been allowed to investigate the crime scene. Time and time again, Vince told him that it wasn't even his jurisdiction.

Things began to get heated the second the sheriff walked through the door. He had been getting settled in when Glen called him and, with no time to get anything done, he hopped into his truck and drove down towards Glen's shack. Only to get a call when three quarters of the way there telling him that he had no need to go there for obvious reasons.

Add on top of that that Sheriff Eugene Winslow didn't particularly care for Vince Warner and that Glen was a resident in the community that he tried to keep under control and he became agitated.

"I just don't understand why I couldn't help," Sheriff Eugene Winslow stated. "It sounded like you needed at least a second pair of eyes out there. Maybe then someone would've seen the body being taken away into the river."

"I can handle my job, Sheriff. If you really are that concerned, then you can take it up with our delightful mayor and see what she wants to be done."

"This just doesn't make sense. How can you be in control of an area away from my department's prying eyes?"

"The thing is, Sheriff, I own part of the land that I allow Glen and his hunters to stay on. I decide what happens on it and who can go tramping around in it."

"Sounds crooked to me." The sheriff made no effort to hide his distaste.

"Trust me. It's all very legal and nothing shady is going on there."

"I guess time will tell." Sheriff Eugene Winslow turned to walk out the door.

"Oh, and Sheriff!" Vince called to him.

He looked over his shoulder.

"Make sure them tree huggin' hippies stay off my property," he said, more so demanded, and then returned to his paperwork.

***

They entered the cove in awe at its splendor yet again. It was as gorgeous as ever with the overhanging branches and the willow trees sprinkled around the atoll. The plot of soaked land itself seemed to be drying quickly under the searing sun but it still needed more time.

However, time was not what the group had. Tanner was the first to don the muck boots and hop off onto the soggy dirt. The rest followed suit and they made their way towards the center of the atoll.

"Alright, gang. Let's see what else this chunk of land brings us today. Tomorrow, we'll head further into the mangroves."

They all feigned glee in unison.

Everyone but Tiffany began to ascend to the top of the atoll. She decided to check the water for the supposed man-eater. Unsure what to expect, maybe the gator from yesterday, maybe nothing, however she did want to check the nets as well. Maybe there'd be something cool in there.

Dallas and Mitch had set them up before they left yesterday. There was bound to be something in there. Tiffany would settle for an oyster. She'd prefer one with a pearl inside but beggars couldn't be choosers.

She stepped into the muddy water with her boots making a squelching sound. As she pressed on further, the water was soon up to her knees. All of a sudden, her foot got stuck. There was a fleeting sense of fear as if she would be unable to free her foot. Returning to a calm sense of rationality, she tried again to walk forward. Instead, her foot came out of the boot and she fell forward into the water.

Grabbing for anything to support herself, she felt around. Suddenly, there was something somewhat sharp. It poked her and she retracted her hand with a quick yelp. The pathetic scream was loud enough to alert the others who came running to her aid.

Tiffany was unwilling to wait for them to help her. She reached out again and found something, presumably a log, to help her up. Using all her might, she pushed up. Her hand slipped into some sort of crevasse that felt chunky and she fell back and pulled with her a hideous sight. What she had thought was a log with a sharp branch protruding out of it proved to be a dead body with a hand that had nail extensions.

Now she screamed loud.

***

The body of Juanita was pulled from the water by Sheriff Eugene Winslow and Vince Warner. The officer had been thankful that he had decided to go back into the fish and game warden's office to settle things because he was able to hear the call. Had he not been there, there was a chance he never would have been notified.

The six conservationists or activists, or whatever they called themselves, were starting to get on Vince's nerves. First they had been talking with Glen yesterday while he was losing it, then he saw them this morning talking to him down by the dock. If they got the wrong idea, it could make things very difficult for his business.

Tiffany was being cradled in Mitch's arms while Lola, Dallas, Kyle, and Tanner were with the sheriff answering some questions. Vince walked over after leaving the coroner to exam the body. He noticed that Dallas had a twang to it and he wondered why anyone would presumably name their kid Dallas if they were living in Texas. It seemed kind of on-the-nose.

What was even more interesting was that Dallas seemed to understand the gravity of the situation as much as the others. Vince wanted to shake the stereotypical thought from his head but couldn't help but think of those old cowboy movies where the western heroes would be familiar and unfazed by death.

He then turned his attention to the Australian. He tried to remember her name. In the end, it didn't matter to Vince. She was a bombshell with blonde hair, striking dark blue eyes, a buxom chest and straight figure. He had heard people say that most women don't look like the magazines portray, especially from Australia. However, she proved them all wrong.

Then there was Kyle and Tanner. Kyle was a bit scrawny and had very short brown hair. His glasses kept sliding down his face and he had a nerdy appearance. Yet he spoke with authority and dignity. More than any man of his stature should feel capable of doing. All the while Tanner was taller, had a nice wave to his hair, blue eyes and a beard. He seemed more the adventurous type with the strong body and deep voice. Yet he sensed vulnerability from him. He couldn't quite figure it out.

He then turned his attention to the two sitting on a log on shore. Mitch was much like Kyle in figure but seemed to have his wits about him. Maybe he was quick on his feet, he couldn't quite tell. Tiffany seemed like a princess with thin dirty blonde hair and a pink hairband atop her head. *Might as well be a tiara,* he thought. Her hazel eyes, innocent face, and small hands made her look cute yet possibly dangerous. She seemed like the person who could take advantage of anyone.

After taking them all in and assuming their traits, Vince decided to hop in the conversation which seemed to be leading into calling the mayor.

"Whoa, guys. I'm sure she doesn't want to be bothered."

"She's going to want to be involved with this, Warner," Sheriff Eugene Winslow said. "Besides, it'd be in her best interest if she wants to get a handle on this thing."

"Whatever you say, Sheriff," Vince said.

Sheriff Eugene Winslow pulled out his cellphone when he heard puttering. He turned to see a very small boat was making its way over.

"Hey! This is a restricted area! Turn back now!" Vince shouted before the sheriff could.

Soon, Glen Porter came into view, as did Oliver Jones and a couple of other men. Sheriff Eugene Winslow recognized Carlos and Stanley immediately. The boat did not slow. Instead, it entered right through the cove entrance until its hull brushed up against the sand.

"Well well well, Sheriff. Looks like that makes two dead now," Glen grinned. "Three if you count my good friend Richard Stillwell."

No one said a word for a short while.

"When are you putting the bounty out?" Oliver asked sternly. "I need the money to buy my daughter a new pair of shoes for school."

"I'll do no such thing until we're one hundred percent certain what this animal is. I can't have you four or others hunting down everything that moves in the everglades, now can I?"

Stan, another hunter, chuckled at that. "Why not? It's pretty much fair game out there now anyway."

"Limitations will be kept on what can be hunted and how much. Right now, I've got to deal with two dead bodies and a coroner's report." Sheriff Eugene Winslow looked at the man in question.

The coroner stood up and, without missing a beat, came to his conclusion. "The bites on both victims are identical. I have no doubt in my mind that Samuel Powers was bitten in half and then finished off later and Juanita was chewed, swallowed, and excreted by a crocodile... and a big bastard at that."

"Shit," the sheriff cursed under his breath.

"Then it's settled; open season on crocodiles!" Carlos chimed in.

Oliver started up the boat.

"Don't you forget that there are differences between crocodiles and alligators, boys," Sheriff Eugene Winslow called to them. "Ya hear me?!"

As if to reply, they shot off a few rounds into the air. They soon turned around a bend and were gone. The water settled and everything returned to the norm. If by norm it meant a dead body and a killer crocodile on the loose then yeah, it was an average Tuesday. The sheriff was getting one of his migraines.

Turning to face the group of students, Vince Warner, and the coroner, Sheriff Eugene Winslow made a statement he'd promised before. "Alright, let's call the mayor."

He knew she'd understand and be scared for the community and wildlife. However, he hated to bother her on such a nice day. Still, this was urgent and he began to dial.

CHAPTER SIX

It was always the same.

No matter how hard she tried, she could not get a tan. Lounging on the deck of her yacht in a black bikini, Emma Darwin reminded not only herself but the rest of the world that she was a bombshell at forty. Not that she tried to do so. It just came naturally.

The sun beat down relentlessly on the deck but she didn't break a sweat. She had started a new diet earlier this year and it was working wonders. Never had she thought she'd be so fit. She hadn't ever been chubby either though.

She brushed a hand through her soft wavy red hair and opened her dark brown eyes. The sun wasn't directly on her so she could still see without having the need to shield her eyes. Deciding to sit up, her two huge breasts instantly fell back into place. She was grateful they were implants and not the real thing, otherwise, she'd be having even worse back problems.

Turning towards the cabin, she got up and went inside. Sliding the glass door with a swooshing sound that she attributed to fine craftsmanship, Emma went to go check her phone. It had three missed calls on it. There was one from her father and two from the sheriff. She had to come to a decision and weighed what was more important; her father's requests and suggestions or the sheriff and the town. It wasn't a hard choice.

She dialed a ten-digit number and the phone began to ring. It rang for a good several seconds and Emma wondered if he'd ever pick up. Finally, a shuffling noise could be heard followed by a voice. He was talking with someone else before answering.

"Hello?" Emma said, a bit annoyed.

"Hey Emma, we've got a problem down here."

"What's going on, Eugene?" Since they weren't being formal, she decided not to call him sheriff.

"I've got two dead bodies now. One was found on a beach torn in two while the other, Juanita, was stuck in a net. Both have identical bite marks and their wounds match those of a croc attack."

Emma was beside herself. She had known about Samuel Powers but prayed that Juanita would be found alive. Instead, one out-of-towner and a citizen were dead. She carefully began to plan out what to do in her head. "Let's make sure this doesn't happen again, Eugene. I'm going to have a press conference to warn people to be wary of the ocean and to stay out of the everglades."

"Alright, so I take it hunting down the croc is in full effect?" Eugene asked but he already knew the answer.

"You bet," Emma said.

With that, they ended the call and Emma called back her father. His gruff voice answered the phone immediately. *"Emma, where have you been? I called you twenty minutes ago!"*

Emma turned her gaze towards the deck of her yacht and gave an uneasy smirk. "I was handling something. What's up?"

"I just wanted to check in to see how the investigation is going."

Emma began to wonder how her father found out things so fast with no information leaked to back it up. Gregory Darwin was a man not to be trifled with and he always knew. That's all she ever chalked it up to being. Still, she played dumb.

"What   investigation?"

"You know damn well what investigation. Samuel Powers' death has impacted Darwin Industries greatly. Lest we forget he had a hand deep in his pockets to fund our research."

There was a momentary pause.

"We know he's dead, as is a woman called Juanita."

"That's nice. Do we know what killed them?"

Emma was taken aback by his disregard for Juanita's life. It took her a few seconds to recover. "It was a crocodile."

There was no response. Instead, her father hung up the phone without so much as a goodbye.

***

Business had proved to be flourishing over the past year. The sales had been good despite the raised prices, the place was kept spotless, and the customer satisfaction rates were through the roof. Most, if not all, of that had to do with Mary.

With her perfect figure, dazzling smile, and buxom chest, she kept the consumers coming back all week. She outdid all the other waitresses and waiters in tips. This was thought to cause a problem with the rest of the employees which would lead to a strike. However, Mary had a solution to this. Give each of the three other employees a quarter of her tips. That way they'd all make the same amount.

She was a beautiful person inside and out.

The perfect prey.

Mary had decided to stay late at the Gills 'n' Grill to finish cleaning up the restaurant. After the group of six friends had left, a rowdy bunch of tourists took their place. They made a mess of the biggest dining table and didn't leave until a minute after closing.

As much as she loved her job, Mary knew that times were getting tough. Still, she held out for a manager position. Tara was leaving soon and she was the leading candidate – a picture perfect example of the picture perfect employee. It'd make having to deal with messy customers easier. She wouldn't have to clean up after them anymore.

When the tables were spotless and the empty trays and glasses washed, Mary went to take off her apron. She began thinking of that one handsome guy who seemed to be wrapped around that other woman's finger. *Too bad,* she thought. *He wasn't too shabby looking.* With the last of the knot coming undone, she suddenly remembered something.

"Oh drat; the trash!" She quickly redid her apron and grabbed the black bag.

As she made her way towards the door, she could swear she heard a low growl. She didn't pay it much attention however, instead opting to turn on the outside light. When she opened the door, she was quickly reminded about why she hated to do this particular job.

The trash wouldn't be taken to the dump until tomorrow afternoon. Building up in a putrid pile, the bags were stacked at least five feet high next to the already full dumpster. She had to place the full bag next to it, starting a brand new pile.

She turned to head back inside. While unfastening the apron again, she heard a squelching sound. A sudden thought crossed her mind. *What if it was that guy from earlier?* The thought of him taking advantage of her atop the freshly cleaned tables turned her on ever so. She spun around expecting to see him. Instead, a slowly extending pair of jaws began to widen in front of her. Stumbling, she fell back into the trash bags. The smell was as ghastly as that thing's breath.

Quickly getting to her feet while in a fit of coughing, Mary ran for the door. A huge tail came down in front of it, blocking her escape. The whole ground shook and a nearby lantern on a pole jiggled. She didn't think twice and, instinctively, hopped over the scaly object.

Without a moment to spare, the crocodile raised its tail and eventually it settled back into place behind it. On the way, however, it brushed against a pole, knocking the lantern down onto the ground. The dry grass next to it immediately caught fire.

Mary could only scream in fear as the shadow of the crocodile, teeth and all, disappeared from view. She then suddenly realized that the shadow was created by the dancing flames. There was no time to ponder on it anymore. She had to get out of there.

Her blood ran cold when she saw the door frame she just ran through start to turn a bright orange. The fire soon shot through it. Deciding the choice way to escape would be the front of the restaurant, Mary charged for that particular exit.

Smash!

The whole roof caved in and the dreaded scaly tail landed on the floor in a splintery explosion. Thankfully, none of the wood had hit her but she was now frozen in fear. She didn't want to risk her life by jumping over the tail again. Besides, it'd probably just lift up again and take her with it.

Instead of what she thought would happen, the tail sort of slithered out of the building. It moved at a snail's pace but, eventually, it was outside. Now was her chance, she could escape. If she only had the ability to move from her frigid state; there would be salvation.

Several seconds passed, the tail did not return. She managed to pick her head up and see through the roof and out into the starry night. The sky reminded her of her innocence as well as her vulnerability, especially as a child. Back then, she felt so tiny and defenseless. After getting into the working world, it seemed nothing could stop her. The idea that a force of nature would be her downfall caused her to begin to tear up. She didn't know what to do.

Suddenly, the room began to get very hot. She could hear the growl coming from outside like a deep echoing purr. The beast had won. Slowly, she admitted defeat by balling up into the fetal position. The fire soon reached her. Her red dress with the white polka dots was the first to catch flame. The sound of her skin sizzling and the smell of her flesh boiling didn't make her scream though. Not until her hair caught fire did she begin to cry and screech into the smoke-filled starry night.

***

It had been snowing when he lost everything. His job, the love of his life, and his will to live – all stricken from him in one swift notion. He had been a captain on a whale watching trip and a damn good one too. Even though he'd been told to follow a certain path, he knew that he had to entertain his audience with as much mammal action as possible.

He took his own courses.

However, one course in particular led to disastrous results. The whale watching yacht ran into a mighty storm that had already shifted its predicted direction. The vessel capsized and seven people were killed. Whether it be by impact with the boat or drowning, they all lost their lives.

Fired and charged with manslaughter, the case was soon dropped due to lack of evidence. People went into an uproar, including those who were on the boat when it happened.

The trial went from late summer to mid-winter. The trial ended in March with the results. Vince Warner had said that he was given incorrect coordinates and had tampered with his directions before leaving the ship. Others were held accountable but his bosses and even his wife knew better. The last snow storm came and went with everything he had.

Somehow, someway, somewhere along the line, he managed to get a job as a fish and game warden. Some said that he bribed people while others said that the higher ups felt pity for him. Regardless, here he was, Graceville, Florida. On the cusp of the everglades is where he sat and watched the sunrise along with smoke in the distance.

He had been the first to call in the fire. However, this time, it wasn't in his jurisdiction. Sheriff Eugene Winslow had to be notified. Dreading dialing the numbers, Vince eventually did so and he heard the ringing. It reminded him of all the times he tried to reach his ex-wife. However, this time, the other end was picked up.

Sheriff Eugene Winslow had slept at his desk all night. The idea of two people found brutally mauled near his town didn't sit right with him. The crocodile would eventually make its way towards Graceville and then they'd all be in real trouble.

He opened his crusty eyes when he felt a familiar vibration. Reaching down, he pulled his cellphone out his pocket. It was odd to be getting a call this early in the morning but he answered it nevertheless.

The relaxed voice of Vince Warner asked for him to look out his window and towards the water. Eugene didn't feel like playing games this morning. "What is it, Warner?"

"There's a fire near the water's edge. Around where the Gills 'n' Grill is."

Sitting straight up, Sheriff Eugene Winslow rushed to his window. His face instantly took on a look of full-colored horror. He was as white as a ghost. He rushed back to his desk and spoke into the phone gravely. "It isn't near the Gills 'n' Grill... It is the Gills 'n' Grill."

CHAPTER SEVEN

Embers fell.

Landing on the ground with a hiss, they danced in the sky as they rose with the pushing flame. Descending to the earth, they turned from bright orange to a crispy ash. It was almost like steel to water except they didn't make things stronger. Enough of them would cause another small fire to grow.

The Gills 'n' Grill had been off the beaten path. It was a hotspot (literally now) but was easy enough to gain access to. However, when the fire trucks tried to enter, they found it hard to get a good spot due to the mangroves and mud. Eventually, two of them just stopped and six firefighters converged on the scene.

Water began to douse the building but it was already proving to be difficult for the foreseeable future. It was burning the ground around the building. Patches where dry grass used to be were now just pockets of flames.

More sirens could be heard as Sheriff Eugene Winslow, Deputy Frank Gaston, and other officers of the law arrived at the encroaching flames. The restaurant hadn't seen this much action since its early days.

One of the firefighters approached Sheriff Eugene Winslow and Deputy Frank Gaston. They explained that the water tanks were close to empty and they'd need to resort to using the river. The sheriff gave them the green light and the alternative measure was taken.

Out of the corner of Sheriff Eugene Winslow's eye, he caught sight of a van approaching the scene. It had a familiar design and color. He then recognized it as the activists' or conservationists, or whatever they called themselves.

As the van came to a stop, the sheriff personally approached them. "You need to get out of here!"

"What happened here, Sheriff?!" Tanner asked while sounding genuinely concerned.

"There's a fire that needs to be put out right now. That's all you need to know."

"We were just here yesterday morning! How could this happen?" a woman's voice, Australian, sounded from the back.

"Look, just head back into town. There'll be a press conference meeting later today," the sheriff explained.

It then dawned on him that he hadn't alerted Emma yet. She was getting a meeting set up with the hunters that she had been putting off. He figured they'd just have to wait longer.

"Go!" The sheriff waved the group off angrily.

Tanner backed up and drove behind some shrubs.

"What're you doing?" Lola asked.

"This'll affect the environment on a staggering level. I want to be there when the fire's out to get some samples," Tanner explained.

Lola shook her head in annoyance and then looked out the window. She saw a man standing in the marshland. Glen Porter! "Hey, look!" she shouted.

Dallas and Tiffany looked but Mitch seemed too preoccupied with staring at the burning building.

"Well well well, if it isn't our Cajun friend," Dallas said with his Texan drawl.

"What is he doing out here?" Tiffany asked no one in particular. "He's creepy."

Tanner and Kyle looked back to see that Glen was now moving towards the scene of the fire. They kept watching him as he emerged from the brush. They all expected for him to be shooed away. However, the sheriff turned, saw him, and then redirected his attention to a firefighter he was speaking to.

"Locals before outsiders, I guess," Kyle said.

They then saw the sheriff pull out his cellphone and begin to dial a number.

***

Any excuse would do.

For Emma Darwin, focusing on this minute issue was tasking her patience. As Oliver Jones stood in front of a group of fifty, way more than the other day, he had a smug look on his face. That ate her up even more.

Accompanying her was her two bodyguards and a secretary. They didn't look particularly thrilled either. Suddenly, the secretary's phone rang and they answered it. At least she'd have a moment of reprieve.

Then there was a tug at her arm. Emma looked back and saw that one of her guards was pulling at her black suit. She gave a confused look but then thought better of it. They made their way back into the building. All the while the hunters were outraged.

Emma took the phone from her secretary. "Emma Darwin."

"Emma, it's the sheriff. We've got a big problem here. The Gills 'n' Grill is on fire. One of the firefighters who eats here says that it doesn't look like the flames have reached the oil tank yet but..." Sheriff Eugene Winslow was cut off.

"Sheriff..?" Emma asked.

The response took a few seconds. "I'm still here, Mayor. A firefighter said that they may be able to contain it. Can you meet us down here?"

She began to question what they needed her there for but thought no harm could come of it – especially if the fire was almost put out. "I'll be right there."

The chauffeur was waiting by the limousine by the time they went out the side of the building. The hunters could be heard marching around the front of the town hall. They were making their way around. Still, the driver managed to evade them.

Emma sat back and took a few moments to process what had happened. She had dodged a second meeting with the hunters. However, in order to do that, a building had to be burning. What was next?

***

The fire had died down to the point where people in the appropriate gear could make their way through the rubble. Firstly, the lantern was discovered. It was pinpointed as the cause of the problem. That along with a few scales in the dining area, made it even more clear what had happened.

Over the radio, the firefighters explained their theories. One was that the crocodile came in search for food and knocked over the lantern. However, there was no dry husk of a reptilian body anywhere to be found. The second, and more probable theory, was that the crocodile went inside to attack someone or something and managed to escape while knocking over the lantern. This theory became more validated when they found the burnt body of Mary.

Still in a fetal position, cradling her crispy knees, Mary was burnt to a crisp. No hair on her beautiful head or clothes covering her beautiful body could be seen. As a firefighter carried her out, Mitch got a good first look at the woman he had been trying to flirt with the day before.

The van door slid open and he ran towards the bushes. Vomit expelled from him like all the possible emotions he felt for her.

"I wish I had my camera," Tiffany said nonchalantly.

Mitch slowly turned his head towards the van. "What did you say?"

"Well, people pay big bucks for this kind of shit. Snuff and stuff... hey, that rhymed!"

"Yer one sick puppy," Dallas said coldly.

"What?! I didn't kill her!" Tiffany just didn't get it.

"I can't believe you're even going there," Mitch said as he walked past the van and towards the crime scene.

Sheriff Eugene Winslow was about to object when he saw the grave look on the young man's face. He figured he knew her and just let it go.

A tarp was laid out and the body of Mary was placed on it. Mitch knelt down next to it. He felt that he loved this woman but they had only met for no more than ten minutes. *One more minute could've led to a lifetime of happiness.* He shuddered at his mistake. *Maybe if I had been here with her last night and not hanging out with Tiffany, she'd still be alive.* Eventually, he pulled himself together, got up, and made his way back to the van.

Haunted, Mitch felt responsible for the death of Mary. He was so absorbed in his thoughts that he didn't see the limousine pull up behind the van. Thankfully, the driver did see him and stopped on a dime.

Tanner opened the driver's side door and helped Mitch stumble inside. He then shut the door and looked over. He saw the driver get out of the elongated car and open the passenger's side door. Emma Darwin got out and Tanner felt a surge of emotion fill within him.

He was about to say hello to the stunning looking woman when her phone rang. She turned in her place and walked towards the crime scene. Tanner felt then that the timing was inappropriate anyway given his friend's current state. He got back into the van and they made a small U-turn and drove out of there.

Meanwhile, Gregory Darwin began the conversation with one simple question. "What the hell is going on down there in Graceville?!"

"How do you find out about these things so fast?" Emma asked her father.

"Just answer the question."

"Well, Dad, it's like this. We've had three murders now," Emma began as she stood over the corpse of Mary. "Not to mention a burnt down restaurant, angry hunters, and oh did I forget to mention a giant fucking crocodile?!"

"Alright, calm down," Gregory demanded.

"What should I do, Dad?" she pleaded for help.

Her father did not change his tone. "Hold that meeting with the hunters. Tell them to forget all about the hippies. Take down this croc and any other croc in the region."

"… And what about the beaches?"

"Leave them open."

"Dad, the crocodile is at the edge of the everglades. It'll be in the open ocean before we even have a chance to see it."

"Ye of little faith." She could see her father smiling from behind the phone.

"I need more faith than what I've gotten from you."

There was a click. No goodbye, just a hang up. She had her orders as far as he was concerned, that much Emma knew. She let her cellphone fall to her side and she struggled to keep her pasty white skin from turning red.

Sheriff Eugene Winslow approached her. "I take it the hunt is on?"

"Yep."

"Anything else I should know?"

"The beaches are staying open."

Sheriff Eugene Winslow was taken aback. That was something he didn't expect. "Who was that on the phone with you?"

"My father."

"That explains it." The sheriff shook his head as he walked by.

Emma could only stand there and contemplate before the blackened building. There was so much going down in this area. Yet, she had to answer to her father constantly. He was making all the wrong decisions for the town and all the right ones for his future. She could only hope that she was included in any plans he had. If he was setting all this up for her bimbo sister, she would let him have it. There was no question about that.

A chunk of building fell away from itself and landed on the ground. The sound of metal framework bending hurt her ears.

This was once a nice place to eat.

She had her orders.

CHAPTER EIGHT

All had remained quiet.

After a day of hunting, Oliver Jones, Glen Porter, and the rest of the gang had turned up what they feared most – nothing. In the early dawn, they drove back out. One party led by Oliver rode across the ocean surface while the other, led by Glen, scoured the everglades. No brush was left to be combed through by the time Glen was done.

The ocean was a harder one to keep track of. There were no mangroves where she could be hiding. Instead, they had to hope that she'd just show up. It was a fifty-fifty chance that she'd pop out of anywhere really. Oliver was beginning to lose hope.

For a second day of hunting, it turned up much like the first. They had nothing. With Emma getting pressured from her father to stop the hunt, everyone thought that she'd give in. However, to their surprise, she was adamant about finding the killer crocodile. For that, they gained newfound respect for her.

One thing none of them had real control over was closing the beaches or even the everglades. With the ever-present threat of the reptilian menace, kids were warned by their parents not to go near the water. Still though, some people dared to venture close. Not just kids. Young adolescents and even full-grown adults made bets about who could wade out the furthest into the water. It wasn't long until some adults thought they saw the crocodile, however, it turned out to be a log.

Deep in the everglades, Tanner and his team still worked. They had shifted their area to a more open section of the river. The atoll was proving to be dangerous what with the gator, the eggs and then a dead body. It wouldn't take much persuasion to have them work somewhere else.

They settled on a stretch of river that ended on a strip of land with plenty of tide pools and vegetation to make a proper analysis on the impact the area had been facing. Even though Tanner didn't want to be labeled an activist, he could not deny that the level of pollution was atrocious.

On the third day with no sign from the crocodile, Sheriff Eugene Winslow approached the group. He looked at the six of them and decided that they were in way over their heads. "You shouldn't be poking around in the swamp so much."

"We can take care of ourselves, thank you," Tanner explained.

"Besides, that crocodile hasn't been seen in a few days. It probably moved on or something. Maybe it was scared off by the fire?" Kyle suggested.

Mitch twitched ever-so-slightly at the thought of Mary. Tiffany noticed but didn't say anything. He wouldn't talk to her regardless; especially not after what she said. Tiffany just had a big mouth and didn't know how to shut it sometimes.

"I don't know," the sheriff continued. "The town's in an uproar. People are scared, hunters are prepping, and politicians are confused. It's just a mess."

"What about Mrs. Darwin?" Tanner asked.

"It's miss; she's not married. And to answer your question, she takes her orders from her father over at Darwin Industries. I'm not sure how that works but, apparently, he also has a hand in the political side of things for Graceville."

Just then, Sheriff Eugene Winslow's face lit up. It was as if he had forgotten something and just remembered it. "By the way, Ms. Darwin would like to schedule a meeting with you all."

"When works for her?" Tanner asked.

"Well, she has a town meeting at three o' clock today. How about right after?"

"We'll be there." Tanner smiled.

The sheriff nodded and then walked back to his patrol car. The shell of a man had to slowly get into his vehicle. There was an obvious stress on his joints and on his mind.

Tanner turned to the group. "We'll have to cut our studies short today."

"I wonder what she wants," Lola stated.

"I'm sure it's nothing that we can't handle," Tanner chuckled.

His positive reinforcement made the group groan. Still, they made their way to the fan boat and didn't complain anymore once they were on the river.

***

After a long night of thoroughly scanning the everglades, Glen Porter decided to take the morning to get some stuff done at his shack. There was no time for sleep for him. This was personal.

Taking a hammer to steel, bashing it into a straight form, he decided then and there that he'd shove the blade into the crocodile's eye. If that failed, he'd shoot her in the same spot, hopefully hitting the brain and ending his constant nightmares.

They were always the same kind of dream. He and Richie, fishing in a dark mangrove, were always being attacked by the black-scaled monstrosity. It only really happened once but it lived on in Glen every other night. Sometimes, night after night even.

Snapping and cracking sounds became almost annoying by this point but unsettling nevertheless. The breaking of Richie's bones haunted him. He could still hear them now even though he was awake. They sounded muffled in the background, almost as if it was happening underwater.

He slammed the hammer onto the orange tinted blade over and over until it was straight enough. *One more whack oughta do it,* Glen thought as he brought the blunt object down onto the thin blade again.

Snap!

It had been one hit too many. The blade snapped in half and the top part fell to the white sandy floor. Glen cursed under his breath. He then looked at the watch on his wrist. It was his grandfather's and constantly needed to be fixed. However, it read quarter to ten and, judging by the sun, he believed it.

There was still time to forge another one.

Another blade to end the crocodile's fury is all he had time for. Even if he arrived late to the hunt, Glen knew that he'd finish her off. Then he could sleep in peace again.

***

The dreaded podium was the last place Emma Darwin wanted to be right now. Normally she wouldn't have any problem addressing the issues at hand. However, with a majority of the townspeople wondering why the restrictions were put up, she had to say something. She would rather have just stuck with reporting to the hunters when she had the chance.

This was going to be big.

As she walked across the stage, the outside sun beating on her pasty skin, she noticed a group of young adults standing off to the side. Four men and two women, all of whom looked tired. She instantly deduced that they were the conservationists, activists, whatever Eugene was calling them. Emma had asked for them to be there and at least they weren't late.

For what it was worth, she at least thought the man in the front was kind of cute. He had wavy brown hair that was down to his neck. It even curled on the ends. His piercing brown eyes stared into hers and she felt something of a connection. It was almost cosmic in a way.

It was hard but she managed to look away and to focus on her duties at hand. Finally approaching the podium that she dreaded so much on this occasion, she adjusted the microphone to be at her preferred height. She wasn't a very tall woman; no more than five foot five. Still, she had a commanding presence over the men. Although, it might've just been her cleavage hanging out that had caught their wandering eyes.

"Ladies and gentlemen of Graceville, for about three days now, we've had a bit of a problem out in the everglades. This might not concern some of you right now but, in the near future, it could become more of an issue."

No one said a word.

"We have reports based on scientific evidence of a crocodile roaming in the everglades and near the oceanic border. Now, I'm sure we can all remain calm but, as a precaution, the ban on all water activities in the everglades is still in effect." She took a deep breath. "… and that goes for the beaches too."

That caused uproar.

Citizens and reporters asked questions alike. They were akin to the event at hand. Some people wondered how long while others, namely the journalists, asked if the crocodile and the fire at the Gills 'n' Grill had any connection.

Sheriff Eugene Winslow waited for Emma's signal to approach the stage and try to take control of the situation. However, to his and the conservationists' surprise, she held her head high. She showed no signs of panic or stress.

"Everybody remain calm, please. I'll answer your questions as I call upon you."

Some listened but not everyone. The shouting was too great and the overwhelming responses were baffling. Some cursed as Emma and others seemingly were barking orders. No one saw that coming. Emma didn't realize that closing the beaches as a safety precaution would be so infuriating to the citizens that she had come to know. She began to wonder if her father had been right when her phone rang. "Speak of the devil."

The mass anger continued on even as Emma told everyone to report to Sheriff Eugene Winslow and Gregory Darwin as she got off the stage.

She walked right past Tanner and his group as she answered her phone. Her fragrance made Tanner swell into a blissful nirvana.

"Yes, Dad?" Emma said over the phone.

"*I warned you about this.*"

"I know, Dad. I think I can handle this though. I'll have Eugene set out with the hunters now."

"This'd better work, Emma. Otherwise you might not have a political future."

"What?" She was about to press further.

There was a click and then the cellphone hung up.

"Son of a bitch!" Emma cursed.

"Is everything alright?" Tanner asked from behind.

Emma turned to face him and almost blushed. "Um, yeah," she lied. "Everything's fine. You must be Tanner."

Tanner extended his hand. "The one and only."

She took it gently and shook it.

"This is my brother Kyle and my protégés if you will." He smiled. "This is Dallas, Mitch, Lola, and Tiffany." He gestured to each one of them as he named them.

"This is great. Hey, listen. Do any of you know how to work a camera or any other similar equipment by chance?"

"Lola and Tiffany are your go-to girls."

Emma gave her award winning smile. "That's wonderful. Would you all follow me to my office please? I have a proposition I'd like to discuss with you." The group followed her inside the building. Tanner couldn't stop staring at her red hair and nice rear end. Kyle had noticed Tanner's fascination with her right away but now even Dallas and Mitch were picking up on it. They gave little sniggers here and there.

Soon, they were in Emma's office. She offered them a seat and drinks. They all took a seat but didn't ask for anything more.

As the ceiling fan rotated wobbly, it didn't have much effect on the muggy room. Still, Tanner couldn't help that Emma looked amazing even with all her make-up and hair products in their respective places. He began to wonder as she strode around her desk if she was over the age of thirty.

Emma placed a video camera on her office desk with care. It was a bit bulky as it was probably state-of-the-art. Still, Lola and Tiffany couldn't help but admire it in all its awkward and presumably cumbersome design.

"That must've cost you at least ten thousand," Lola stated.

"Closer to twenty." Emma smiled.

"And what exactly do you want us to do with this camera?" Kyle asked.

It was a reasonable question but Tanner glared at him as if annoyed. Kyle noticed and immediately knew that he had embarrassed him. He figured he wouldn't be a good brother if he didn't keep it going. "I mean, we're not really doing anything all that exciting."

Tanner nudged him with his shoulder.

"On the contrary," Emma began. "You see, the everglades have a beauty to it. However, there has been a darkness sweeping over the river. This crocodile has been causing a lot of problems. Now, before anyone kills it... I'd like to document the creature in its natural environment."

Kyle thought it was ridiculous but Lola, Tiffany, and Tanner seemed more than interested. Dallas didn't want to disappoint either of his employers, old or new. Mitch hadn't said a word since before the meeting.

"Isn't that dangerous?" Kyle asked.

"I don't want you to get an up close shot or anything. Even if you film its supposed nest that'd be more than enough for me," Emma explained to them as if it was no big deal.

"I think we need to discuss this as a group," Kyle said.

"It's not a request to take lightly, for sure. You can let me know in the next couple of hours if you'd like." Emma was trying to seem concerned for their safety. If she was genuine or not, Kyle couldn't tell.

Emma noticed this and tried another tactic.

"Are any of you familiar with firearms?"

Tanner looked her right in the eyes. "I am."

"Me too," Dallas said.

"Well, I expect to see both of you in my office later. I need to go over some stuff with the hunters and it'd be the prime time to equip you with guns. That is if you take the job."

"I'll be there." Tanner smiled.

"Tan, wait. We need to discuss this," Kyle said sharply.

"It'll be alright, little brother. As long as you all are under my watch, I'll see to it that you come out of this unscathed."

"Do we get paid?" Tiffany asked abruptly.

"I'll pay ten thousand for each minute of crocodile footage you present to me; eggs or otherwise."

"Sounds good to me." Tiffany smiled to herself.

"Okay, Tanner, Dallas, meet me back here at two o' clock. We'll hash out all the details."

"Sounds like a plan." Tanner grinned from ear to ear.

Stepping out of the town hall which was stuffy and muggy wasn't all that different than walking outside under the sun with all its humidity. As the group walked down the pavement, Kyle had an irritated look on his face. Tanner didn't pay much attention to it so Kyle decided to speak up. "She's a good lookin' lady, huh?"

"Yeah." Tanner seemed to be lost in his own little world.

"Looks like Tanner's got the hots for the mayor." Dallas chuckled as he tilted his hat to shade himself from the sun's rays.

Tanner didn't even respond.

"She can't be older than thirty," Tiffany said.

"Please," Lola scoffed at Tiffany's observation. "She's probably pushing forty."

"Still looks dynamite though," Dallas chuckled.

Lola seemed a bit offended by Dallas' remark but decided to ignore him in favor of wondering what Kyle was doing. He had stormed off about five feet away from the group.

"Kyle!" Tiffany called for him.

"Hey, Kyle. What're you thinking?" Lola asked.

Kyle stopped dead in his tracks. He remained statuesque for a few seconds before turning around and marching towards them, mainly straight for Tanner. "You have no idea what this bitch is trying to accomplish. She could be on the side of the town and want us gone. Or maybe she wants the footage for nefarious reasons. Any way you slice it, she's bad news."

"Or she could be using it as proof." It was Mitch who spoke up as the voice of reason, much to everyone's surprise.

"Highly doubtful," Kyle said.

"Is it really though?" Mitch continued. "Think about it, the crocodile has killed three people at least and no one's even seen it. It caused a building to catch fire and, lest we forget, no one saw a damn thing until dawn!"

No one debated Mitch's logic.

"It's more likely that Miss Hot-pants is just trying to get proof to acquire extra help. Reinforcements will probably be needed to take out a beast this big."

"Then why ask the town drunks to hunt it down?" Kyle shot back.

"Because there's no guarantee she can get the help. They're all she has right now."

At Mitch's astute observation, Kyle relented and backed down from the argument. "I still think this is fishy."

"More like scaly," Mitch joked.

"That's the Mitch we know and love. Welcome back to the world of humor." Dallas shook Mitch's arm lightly.

The six of them made their way towards the apartment complex. Mitch continued to joke and everyone was careful about their responses. They knew he was still hurting but, as seen before, sometimes comedy is the best coping mechanism for damaged or depressed people.

They laughed all the way towards the entrance of the building. Their last-minute rooms were all situated by a routine maid. Dallas and Mitch entered the first room followed by Lola and Tiffany who were in the middle. Lastly, Tanner and Kyle entered the biggest room. It held all their equipment.

Tanner held his arms out and then fell back on his bed. The cushiony mattress absorbed him and he felt smothered but he didn't mind. He couldn't help but think that Emma was sitting right next to him. He could almost get a whiff of her sweet smell. She had a natural smell of soap that reminded him of honey. He just wanted to hold her and then take things further. Beginning to get aroused, he quickly shot up and turned to Kyle who was sitting on his bed and looking out the window.

"I'm going to get a shower," Tanner said.

"Good, it might clear your head." Kyle didn't seem bothered to put emphasis on his insult.

Tanner paid no mind. He then entered the bathroom and began to disrobe.

***

It was only a few miles away but it might as well have been a thousand. Emma began to take off her black floral dress with the massive V-neck. She then made her way to the bathroom and slipped into the tub with little rippling. She began to rub her body with the soapy water. Her milky white skin shone under the fluorescent lights above. She loved the feeling of her soft skin. It was titillating. She secretly wished she had a man to do it for her. The excitement of intimacy brewed deep. Though there was not much time for a regular life, these desires poked through every once in a while.

Tonight, she could put a name and face to the fantasy. Tanner Felton.

She heard a sudden knock at the bedroom door. It snapped her out of her dreamy state and caused her to get up and quickly reach out for her baby blue silk robe. It was hanging from a hook next to the tub.

"Just a minute," Emma said as she quickly got out of the tub and slipped her robe back on. As she tied a knot in it, she opened the door. It was Sheriff Eugene Winslow.

"The hunters are upset, ma'am," he said quietly.

"I know. I told them two o' clock and I'm sticking to that," Emma continued. "I want Glen, Oliver, Stan and even Vince Warner all present as well. We need to come up with a solid plan of finding this thing and, with all of their knowledge, I'm sure we can come up with something."

She seemed sincere but Sheriff Eugene Winslow could sense that this was just another one of her speeches. "Okay, I'll see to it."

"Thank you, Eugene. Is that all?" she asked, already closing the door slightly.

"Yes, ma'am." He turned and walked away.

***

She may have been incredibly unlikable but Mitch had to admit that Tiffany looked amazing in her dark blue bikini. He had seen her by happenstance as she made her way towards the pool. It was around one o' clock and there would be plenty of time to fool around with her.

There was a nagging feeling in the back of his mind though. His need for her to satisfy his desires was great but he knew that it would be a mistake. There would be no passion, only lust. That wouldn't have been a problem, hell he'd felt that way about Mary, but she had said things that were wildly inappropriate.

Now, after all this teasing, she was sitting by the poolside and seemingly beckoning for him. *What a bitch.* That was the official term he came up with for her.

In a move that made Mitch feel not only better but triumphant, he walked away from the window. He didn't leave through the door, instead he turned on the television and began to drift off into a powernap.

Tiffany couldn't believe it. She had seen him standing by the window and then he walked away. Walked, not ran. She gave him a few more minutes and there was still no sign of him. She lifted her legs out of the water and began to stride towards the door.

She would give him a piece of her mind. How dare he barely acknowledge her. This was unacceptable. She'd pick the right time and place to tell him off.

All these thoughts were in the back of her mind while lust was in the forefront. She wanted Mitch bad. There was a saying that she didn't want to think about yet it kept reforming in her mind. Finally, she unknowingly said it quietly to herself. "You don't know what you have until it's gone."

Not that she'd ever admit to saying or even thinking that. She was too proud of her snooty reputation. Her father paid for this expedition and she'd get whoever her heart desired. This wasn't the end of her and Mitch. It was only their beginning.

***

Everyone was on time, much to Emma's surprise. She had presumed that at least the hunters would've been late. It was stereotypical but not too far off from this particular group's behavior. She was dressed in a grey t-shirt as they stood around her office desk. This was a serious event. However, her casual attire made them feel less scared and more like this was a regular hunt. It gave them confidence or cockiness. Emma couldn't tell.

Glen, Oliver, and Stan stood around the desk with Tanner and Dallas sitting in the chairs in front of it. Laid out before the group were several high-powered rifles and an elephant gun. They almost looked like well-kept antiques but were pristine enough to work. They also looked like they'd pack a real punch.

This gave confidence to Tanner and Dallas who snatched up a pair of the rifles and looked them over. Both of them had scopes, as did pretty much all high powered rifles, and Dallas looked through his and aimed it out the window past Emma. He got a pretty good view out towards the ocean. The clarity was so great that he saw a seagull not only fly by but take a crap on some poor kid's head. He chuckled.

"How's the view?" Tanner asked.

"Shit's fantastic." He smiled.

Oliver and Stan walked up and picked up their respective rifles while Glen made his way for the elephant gun. As he put it under his shoulder, the barrel facing to the floor, he sighed.

"What's the matter?" Emma asked.

"This isn't enough."

"The hell you say?!" Stan exclaimed.

Oliver put his rifle down. "Glen here has seen this crocodile. If he says this isn't enough then I believe him." Stan was hesitant but decided to side with Glen and Oliver on this one. He put his gun back on the desk. "If they say it isn't enough, then I'm with them."

"Gentlemen, this isn't a war room. We don't have a cabinet filled with military grade weaponry," Emma continued. "If you think a crocodile can withstand a headshot from one of these rounds then I'd call your bluff."

"*A* crocodile, no they couldn't. This crocodile though," Glen looked down at the weapons. "I don't feel satisfied, hell, I don't feel safe with these by my side. We'd be barrels blazing as she approached and she'd still get us."

"That's your call, Glen," Emma began. "If you have some better alternatives for taking down this beast, I suggest you present them. Whether it be guns or just ideas."

"You really are that desperate?" Glen smiled.

"Do I have a choice? It's killed three people!"

"Recently; don't forget my good buddy, Richie." Glen was annoyed but didn't show it behind his grin.

"I'm sorry. Four people have been killed by the crocodile."

Glen put the elephant gun on the desk. "That's better."

The three hunters walked out the door. Sheriff Eugene Winslow, who had been silent in the corner this whole time, walked them out of the building. Emma sat down on her leather seat and put her elbows on the desk, rubbing her face with her hands.

"We'll get this animal documented and then destroyed for you, Mayor," Tanner spoke up.

Emma looked up at the two gentlemen and smiled. "God, I hope   so."

Suddenly, the door opened and Glen walked in. He was carrying something in a wrapped cloth. As he approached the desk, Emma became wary. She was about to hit the red button under her desk to alert her bodyguards when Sheriff Eugene Winslow walked in. Her finger still hesitated over the button up until he nodded. It was enough to reassure her that everything was alright.

Glen placed the cloth on the desk which gave Emma the clear to open it. Inside was a red stick with a fuse on the end. She recognized what it was almost immediately.

"Is that dynamite?" Dallas was taken aback.

"It was Richie's. He was dynamite fishing when the croc snatched him from our boat," Glen explained with a grave tone that made his voice somewhat weak.

Emma said what no one expected. Glen and the sheriff included were thinking she'd confiscate it. However, the look of satisfaction in her eyes was evident. She stared at the dynamite with an almost admiring look. "Do you have any more?"

"Lady, I've got a whole case-full back at my shack."

"Bull," the sheriff's voice boomed. "We searched your shack just last month when you were accused of being involved with drugs. There was no sign…"

"You idiots take the sand for granted. Remember, I have no real floor!" Glen chuckled.

"Never mind that, Sheriff." Emma turned to Glen. "Can this take down our killer?"

"Would I lie to you?" Glen gave a sinister smile to the mayor.

Emma knew the real answer. Any other day she would've said yes and had the dynamite confiscated as well as Glen thrown in prison. However circumstances had changed and today was different.

"Do it. Kill the crocodile," Emma said as she wrapped up the dynamite and handed it back to Glen.

"Can do," Glen said, tilting his tan boonie hat.

Sheriff Eugene Winslow decided to not only escort Glen out of the town hall but watch him drive away with Oscar and Stan.

"Is there anything else you need?" Tanner asked.

"No, you can both leave. Thank you," Emma said.

Tanner and Dallas nodded, got up and made their way for the door. Emma couldn't help but stare at Tanner's rear end as he walked. She silently prayed that he was at least thirty.

He hadn't said anything but Tanner did notice through a mirror next to the door that Emma was staring at him longingly. His heart melted. He hadn't felt this way since seeing Rachel McCormick on prom night. He hadn't asked her out and that had been a mistake. There was still a chance to do so with Emma.

In time.

CHAPTER NINE

He was pondering on the past.

Glen Porter had decided to take a small reprieve from the chaos around him and sit on the dock next to his shack. It was only a few minutes before he was lulled into the sounds of the running river. The blue water was contaminated with algae that brushed against the wooden planks from underneath. The aroma of swamp was prevalent but not overbearing. Glen had grown used to this.

Then there was the sound of a car stopping, doors opening, and footsteps approaching. Glen figured out who it was by the sound of their nice dress shoes. He also could tell that there were two pairs of feet making their way over. Four clips, two after the other. They walked in unison.

"Glen," Sheriff Eugene Winslow called.

"Sheriff…" Glen practically mumbled.

"I hope we're not interrupting anything." The sheriff sounded sincere enough.

"Just memories," Glen said as he looked back with a pained expression.

"I just don't get it," it was Deputy Frank Gaston who spoke next. "I mean, how could they let a drunkard be a part of this hunt?"

"No need to heckle the man, Gaston," Sheriff Eugene Winslow said.

Glen didn't pay mind to either one of them and returned to looking out at the river. The sun was getting lower as four o' clock rolled around. He, Oliver, and Stan had decided to hunt tonight. However, it wouldn't be for too long. Oliver had to get back to his daughter and Stan, his dog. Glen decided to go over the plan again in his head, however, in the background, Deputy Frank Gaston was chastising him for his drunken ways.

"Would you knock it off, Deputy?" Sheriff Eugene Winslow was getting particularly annoyed with his officer.

"I mean, the man couldn't stop it when his friend was killed. What chance does he have now?!"

That snapped Glen out of his train of thought, derailed his ideas. He unsheathed a hunting knife from its holster and began to toy with it, placing the tip on his finger and giving it a little twirl. "Five minutes and I can have you ready for the market."

"What did you say, old man?!" The deputy was taken aback.

"Are you unprofessional *and* deaf?" Glen chuckled.

Deputy Frank Gaston went to reach for his handcuffs.

"What do you think you're doing, Deputy?" Sheriff Eugene Winslow demanded.

"He threatened an officer of the law!"

"... And you were harassing a citizen," Sheriff Eugene Winslow stated.

"You're not seriously taking this man's side?!"

"It's not about whose side I take, Frank. It's about doing what's right."

The sheriff's stern glare at his deputy made the latter feel embarrassed. His hand moved away from the cuffs and back to his side. Glen put away his blade and continued to look out at the lazy river.

Sheriff Eugene Winslow ushered his deputy to turn around and go back to the patrol car. He then looked back at Glen. "You might want to not be so close to the edge."

"Roger that," Glen said quietly. He did not budge though.

The officers were driving away when they noticed Glen wasn't on the dock anymore. In fact, they couldn't see him anywhere. There were no ripples in the water so the officers threw out the idea the crocodile got him.

It was after a few minutes of staring that the officers finally saw Glen walking out of his shack. He had a crate with him.

"Shouldn't we be confiscating that?!" The deputy was shocked, especially when Glen opened the contents to reveal dynamite.

"No, he knows what he's doing," Sheriff Eugene Winslow said as he pulled away from Glen's shack and back to Graceville Police Station.

***

The sun was setting as its rays shot across the water. Further and further was its reach. Soon, it was touching the front of Emma Darwin's mansion as she stood there watching it. She admired the pink horizon as the sun made way for night. Dark blue clouds appeared like fluff chasing after the sun. The earth was rotating to night. Emma wished she wasn't alone anymore. She had a fiancé at one point but that didn't work out. Now, all she could do was admire the bright sky turning black. It'd all be over and she'd be back in her bed only to wake up early by herself again.

She often pondered on her career. Knowing that it overtook her social life was one thing. However, her father, Gregory Darwin III, was positioning her into a seat of power that she wasn't sure she was ready for, not even at the age of forty. Still, it was always his way or the highway. That was a fact that became abundantly clear right when she got out high school.

Kids were now a thing of the past. She was past her prime. Still, she yearned for one. She wanted to be able to watch a child of her own grow and have children one day. She didn't want to be the ninety-year-old grandmother.

A single tear was followed by another. This caused a chain reaction. Soon, she was sobbing uncontrollably. Her shiny red lips began to quiver. Finally, she decided that this was not right. She should go in there and tell her father what's for. *To hell with the consequences.*

Walking off her balcony and back into her room, she made for her cellphone. Suddenly, it rang. She was already in the process of dialing and she accidently answered it.

"Hello?" she asked while trying to remain calm.

"Uh, hi is this the mayor's office?"

The man's voice sounded familiar but it was a bit odd coming from the phone.

"Yes, who is this?"

"This is Tanner. We spoke during the meeting briefly." He chuckled.

She blushed uncontrollably right then and there. She felt embarrassed as if he could see her somehow.

"Oh, hi!" she said excitedly and bit her lip carefully to calm herself.

"Is this a bad time?"

"No, you're fine. I was just... watching a sad movie."

"Oh, what was it?"

Emma hoped he didn't ask. She tried to come up with one but fell short. "To be honest, it's just been a hard day."

There was a momentary pause.

"Do you want to talk about it?" Tanner asked, genuinely concerned.

"Not really," Emma said. "I guess it's just all catching up to me. That's all," she said sweetly.

"I get it. We're all under a lot of stress right now," Tanner sighed.

"Is there anything I can help you with?" Emma asked.

"Yeah actually, I was hoping we could discuss a plan I had in private. One that involves the crocodile's destruction."

"It must be illegal if you want to do a one on one with me about it."

Tanner laughed casually. *"How about tonight? We could go somewhere local?"*

"I thought it was to be a private conversation, Mr. Felton."

"Please, call me Tanner. We can just order food if you want?"

There was another pause, longer this time.

"Hello?" Tanner asked, scared that he'd made her uncomfortable.

"How about the local pub, say eight o' clock?"

"Is that really your kind of scene?" Tanner asked.

"Not really, but it'd be private. Everyone keeps to themselves there."

"Okay, that'll work!"

"Great, it's a date!" Emma couldn't believe she said that but Tanner didn't seem fazed by it.

"See you soon, Mayor," Tanner said softly.

"It's Emma, please. And likewise!"

Neither of them hung up right away though. Tanner was about to but decided to hold on a little longer. Emma cradled the phone waiting for him to say something more. *This reminds me of high school in the mid-nineties.* She finally hung up her end.

***

Tiffany was still miffed about Mitch not giving her attention. That kept up even as she walked back from the pool to the shower and eventually the bed. The springy mattress was uncomfortable. She wished she had Mitch or at least some guy to snuggle into on this night. Tossing and turning, she sometimes glanced over at Lola who was, by now, fast asleep.

Her groaning and moaning was getting on her own nerves. Eventually, she couldn't take it anymore and decided to go for a walk.

Outside, the warm Floridian air wasn't as humid anymore. She made her way around the hotel and finally came to the entrance. There, she noticed that the parking lot was missing something. While the crocodile business was going on and the beaches were closed, the tourists decided to pack up and leave. There were five cars left outside this afternoon. Their van was not among them now.

A surge of urgency came about her and she ran for Tanner and Kyle's room. She began to bang on the door which alerted Dallas and Mitch. They both came running out into the hallway just as Kyle opened the door.

"The van's gone!" Tiffany said, panting.

"I know," Kyle said sternly. "Tanner took it to go see his crush."

"Who, the mayor?" Mitch joked.

Kyle just glared at him.

"No way," Dallas said coldly. "That boy's got a set on him, that's for sure."

"Yeah, and I'm sure she'll tell us how big it is sometime. Now, please. I'd like to get some rest," Kyle said while already shutting the door.

Dallas and Mitch were about to go back to their room when Tiffany took Mitch's arm. "Can we talk?"

"I don't know. Can we?" he asked matter-of-factly.

Tiffany looked at Dallas.

"I'll give you guys some space," he said as he walked into the room and shut the door. Tiffany was about to speak when she heard the door lock.

"I guess there's no escape for me," Mitch said.

"Nope," Tiffany said awkwardly.

"What do you want, Tiffany?"

"I've had time to think tonight. I swear, my brain has been doing rollercoaster rides and I'm paying for the admission," Tiffany continued. "I just wanted to say that I'm sorry for being so territorial. I'm also sorry for saying what I did." Mitch gave her a smile then placed a hand on her shoulder. "I forgive you."

Her face beamed.

"Can we talk about this in the morning? I need to get some shut eye."

"Yes, of course. Thank you."

Mitch went to go into his room but the door wouldn't open. "Come on, Dallas."

Tiffany giggled. "See you in the morning, Mitchy."

Mitch turned and saw Tiffany go back to her room. She was gone and he was all alone out in the hallway. Worst of all, he felt a bulge in his trousers. "Seriously, man. Let me in!"

There was no reply.

Lola was still asleep through it all.

***

The pub on 42nd Street was quaint. It was mostly a place for locals and, at first, Tanner felt unwelcome. He began to fidget in his chair and wondered if she'd even show up at all.

Suddenly, there she was. In the doorway to the pub there stood a woman who looked to be in her early twenties. She was beautiful beyond words. Her shoulder length red hair had a nice flowing wave to it. She was wearing a light purple and pink dress. The straps over her arms barely held it in place as her massive cleavage pulled them down. She had glittery high heels on that made a clipping sound as she walked over to his table.

"Hi Tanner." She smiled.

His response was to instinctively get up and pull the chair out for her.

"Such a gentleman," she said as he scooted her in.

A single strand of her hair brushed against his hand and he felt like he was going to lose it right then and there. He kept his composure in check and walked around the table to sit down.

"You look amazing."

"Thank you." Her award winning smile returned.

They didn't even bother looking at the menus. Tanner did notice however that every single guy was staring at her. He wanted to say something but every line he thought of was offensive. So he just held his tongue.

"So, what's your plan?" Tiffany asked excitedly.

Tanner bit his lip and then came out with it. "I don't have one."

"What?"

His next move had to be played right. Tanner was falling for this woman and he wouldn't screw it up. Not like he did with Rachel McCormick.

"I actually wanted to just talk to you."

"Oh? What did you want to talk about with me?"

"I just want to know more about you," Tanner began. "To be honest, Emma, you not only captivate me with your beauty, there's this adorable charm you have that I just want to get to know more. And I can't stop thinking about you. Every time I go to do something, you pop in my head. In all seriousness, Emma, I'm falling for you."

Tanner waited for a quick response but Emma just stared at him. She seemed not to know how to take it. He was about to take it all back when her eyes began to water. She was blushing. Now she was leaning forward. Tanner did the same. Closer and closer until their lips connected.

Emma didn't want to pull away but she heard their server coming and pulled back on instinct.

"Starting dessert a little early, aren't we?" a young waiter said.

"Can I just have a glass of water please?" Emma smiled even though she looked like she was about to cry.

"Sure thing, and for you, sir?"

"I'll have whatever she's having." He didn't even look at the waiter. His eyes didn't want to leave Emma's.

Soon, the waiter came back and asked if they needed anything else.

"A martini please," Emma said. "It's for a special occasion."

"Make that two please," Tanner said.

The waiter smiled. "Can I see some I.D. sir?"

"Come on, man. I'm twenty-five."

The color drained from Emma's face. The waiter noticed this. "My apologies, sir. Two martinis coming up."

Tanner returned his full attention to Emma. "What's wrong?"

Emma didn't know what to say. She was already having a mid-life crisis. There was no need to drag this youthful man down with her. That wouldn't be fair to him. Not to mention all the stuff her father had put her through. "I'm sorry. I can't do this."

She got up and made her way for the door. Tanner chased after her. "Hey, what's wrong?"

"I'm too old for you, Mr. Felton!"

"Since when did we go back to last names, Emma?"

"My point still stands."

"Come on, age is just a number."

"Try fifteen years!" she shouted more than she wanted to.

Much to Emma's surprise and even Tanner's himself, he grabbed her and kissed her again. He thought for sure that she'd pull back but she instead leaned into him. After what seemed like hours, they pulled away from each other. There were no words for a few minutes. They just stared at each other with that same lovey expression from earlier.

"Call me tomorrow," Emma said. "I'll let you know what my decision is then."

Tanner was speechless as Emma got in her car and drove off down the dirt path and onto the highway.

CHAPTER TEN

He slept in the hallway.

Waking with a back cramp, Mitch stood in front of his hotel room door. He chuckled as he figured it was just as comfy as those beds they slept on. After a quick stretch followed by a rolling of his head to pop any cracks, Mitch was up and knocking on his hotel room door. He didn't expect for there to be a response so quickly.

On top of that, he wasn't expecting who ended up answering the door.

Lola's hair was a bit frazzled but looked great nevertheless. Mitch had to admit that he found her more attractive than Tiffany, not only in looks but personality. Still, he knew she had eyes for Dallas and Tiffany would never let either one of them live it down if he pursued his desires.

Dallas soon called out. "Who is it?"

"It's your roommate," she said in her thick Aussie accent.

"Damn, I thought you went with Tiffany last night!" Dallas explained as he got off his bed.

"You didn't hear me knocking?" Mitch asked, flustered.

"No, we were a bit… preoccupied. Didn't you hear us?" Dallas chuckled.

"Nope," Mitch said. "I must have fallen asleep earlier than I thought."

The three of them remained silent.

Finally Mitch remembered something. "I have to take a leak. Can I please come in?"

"Sure, man," Dallas said.

Lola stepped aside as he entered the bathroom.

"Poor guy didn't even go after her," Lola said.

"Smart guy, more like it. I'm sure Tiffany will be super excited to see us this morning." Dallas chuckled again however this time there was a bit of concern in his voice.

None of them wanted to hear of Tiffany's troubles anymore. Nor did they want to feel her wrath. It was too early for that.

Mitch flushed and walked out looking around.

"How'd she even get in here last night?"

Dallas sneered and pointed to a door in the corner of the room. "All we had to do was remove the chairs. Easy access between rooms."

"Well, that's a bit sketchy," Mitch said.

"Not really, a lot of places have them." Lola smiled.

Her smile wasn't one of pity, as if he should've known that. Instead, she seemed happy to tell Mitch of the secret doorways. It was a weird expression but Mitch kind of loved it. Her dazzling smile helped boost his appreciation for it.

Suddenly, Kyle was at the door. He was already dressed in his casual work clothes and taking in the messy room that the three were in.

"Do not tell me you three did something last night that I'll have to hear about later."

"Nah," Mitch said casually. "I just had to come back in, after being locked out all night, to answer the call of nature."

"What?" Kyle asked.

"He had to take a piss," Dallas explained the saying.

"No, I get that. But why didn't you sleep in here unless," he stopped and looked over towards the next room. "Come on, was I the only one that didn't get laid last night?!" Everyone laughed at him.

"Dude, I would've just pissed in their room if I had slept with Tiffany last night," Mitch stated. "I thought you were supposed to be smart!"

"The hell with this! I'm going to get some breakfast. Join me at your leisure," Kyle finished and then stormed off towards the elevator.

***

The hunt brought up nothing. There was no sign of the killer crocodile. Instead, Glen, Oliver, and Stan were treated to silence. This was also odd given the everglades should have been teeming with life during the night. They didn't see any gators, snakes, or any of the abundant wildlife that would've normally been out in the still darkness.

"Feckin' critters are all gone," Glen said as they pulled into the slip.

"Yeah, that was strange," Stan said as he tossed his cigarette into the water.

The dinky boat brushed against the side of the dock. A scraping sound was made that irritated Oliver. Glen knew that it would for it always did hence why he continued to do it every time they came back from a hunt.

Nearby on the shore, an elderly man began to wade into the water. He wasn't afraid, the area was netted off. Even if it wasn't though, Eli Webber would still risk it. He had that kind of don't-give-a-damn attitude ever since his wife passed.

"You're crazy if you think that net will hold 'er back!" Glen called to Eli.

"Forget it, man. He don't care no how!" Stan said as he hopped onto the dock and tied off the small speedboat.

"Ha ha, very funny," Eli then pointed at the water. "Now would you mind shutting up, I'd like to catch a fish today."

The three men got off the boat while trying to remain quiet. There was a respect given to fishermen as old as Eli. He never complained about much, especially not while fishing. There was also the fact that he was the best fly fisherman around. The locations he chose to fish at were another story however. There was a reason he couldn't catch anything. It must have been another side effect of his wife dying – uncaring and unaware.

Just then, Eli tripped on something and fell face-first into the saltwater. Normally Glen would've laughed. However, after seeing all that had been going on, he hopped off the dock and into the cold morning water. He had to swim for it was at least five-feet deep.

As he made his way over, he noticed the water around Eli was turning red. Eli screamed and Glen picked up his pace. It wasn't by much but it was enough.

On the dock, Stan and Oliver trained their rifles on both sides of Eli. They couldn't tell where he had been hit. As soon as Glen had him and was bringing him in, they'd start firing. Both men knew the drill and were ready.

Eli's hand was sticking out of the water and Glen took hold of it. As he pulled the older man up he noticed that there wasn't a scratch on him. Glen looked the man over again and again and then realized that it wasn't his blood.

Oliver and Stan seemed to realize this and, having a higher up view, saw what it actually was. Or rather, who it actually was.

The upper half of Samuel Powers began to float away on the ebbing tide. Eli cursed under his breath while Glen turned to Stan and Oliver.

"Call the sheriff and Warner! They need to see this."

He then turned to face Eli. "Are you okay, old timer?"

Eli nodded. "Looks like I need to find myself a new fishing spot."

***

The blades on the ceiling fan turned slowly as Emma stirred in her sleep. Suddenly, she awoke with a feeling she just had a nightmare. However, just as soon as she had awoken, it had faded from her mind. She turned to look at the empty spot on her bed. She took her hand and ran it across her face.

She felt like a complete idiot.

A ringing sound blared and she turned to see that it was her landline. She hoped it was Tanner but didn't at the same time. Emma spent a good portion of the night thinking about him and yet she still didn't have an answer. Regardless of whoever was on the other end, she picked it up.

"This is the mayor speaking."

"Morning, Mayor," She could tell it was Vince Warner by his annoying voice. *"We've got a bit of a problem."*

"What kind of problem?" Emma placed her hand on her forehead.

"The crocodile kind."

Emma shot up in her bed. *Did the crocodile attack a beachgoer?* She began to feel uneasy. "I'll call Eugene and let him know."

"Already did," Vince Warner said and then the phone clicked.

"Why does everyone hang up on me?" Emma was annoyed and placed the phone back on the cradle.

The phone was an antique and a gift from her father when she got promoted to this job. Admittedly, she didn't know how to place calls on it, only receive. This was the 21st century after all.

Suddenly, the phone rang again and Emma answered it. She had to admit that she liked the sound it made when she picked up and put down the receiver. "Mayor Darwin here."

"Hey, Emma." It was Tanner.

Emma almost choked on nothing. She let loose a gasp that was louder than intended.

"Are you alright?"

"Why do you keep asking me that?" she chuckled.

He didn't answer. Instead, there was an awkward pause. Their conversation lingered in limbo for far too long and Tanner decided to finally say something. *"Did you think about us?"*

"Yes, Tanner. I've been up almost all night."

"Me too. I honestly was hoping you'd call in the middle of the night," Tanner continued. *"I slept in the van. I didn't want to talk to anyone and just needed to be alone with my thoughts. I've thought about us too. I ended up coming to the conclusion that I know what you want about as much as what I want. But I will tell you this… I know I want you in my life."*

Emma was so close to crying that she was biting her lip. "Tanner, you have your whole life ahead of you. There are so many women out there much prettier than me."

"I don't believe that. Plus, they're not as mature and experienced as you are."

Emma chuckled. "Mature, yes. Experienced, not as much as you'd think."

"That doesn't matter. Emma, I really do care for you."

"I just wouldn't feel right about it. Hell, I'm almost old enough to be your mother."

"Please don't do this." Tanner wouldn't admit it but he was on the verge of crying himself.

"I'll talk to you later. I have to go get ready now. Goodbye, Mr. Felton." Emma hung up the phone before he could reply.

She was mad with herself. How could she let things escalate this far? If only he were ten years older. Still, part of her wanted to call him back. It was too late. She knew she'd come across as desperate if she did. Instead, she went into the bathroom, took off her satin light blue robe, and hopped into the shower.

***

It had been a long morning already. Tanner never returned to the hotel and Kyle began to get worried. He called him but he didn't pick up. After a few seconds, he got a text. It read: *go without me.* Kyle felt bad for his older brother but decided to take charge.

"Looks like we're walking to the fan boat."

"Are you fucking kidding me?" Tiffany shouted.

"It's like ninety-eight already and it's a good mile down the road," Lola complained.

"I know, but we have a job to do and Tanner needed to fix the   van."

"Bull, things probably didn't go well with him and the mayor last night and he's taking a day to cool off," Dallas assumed.

His assumption was correct although Kyle wasn't ready to admit that. "Let's just go before it gets hotter."

Inwardly, the group as a whole was just thankful that all the equipment needed for today was already on the boat.

"Don't forget, we're heading a bit outside of the cove today. Best to be safe," Kyle reminded everyone.

"Yes, Tanner... I mean Kyle," Mitch joked.

The five of them walked down the street, onto the pier and soon the fan boat, and were off, going deep into the everglades.

***

The rotted body of Samuel Powers was a bad enough sight. Add on top the fact that he'd been partially devoured and his corpse made for a ghostly image.

Glen, Oliver, Stan and even Eli had remained on the scene. When the cop and fish and game cruisers pulled up, Glen groaned.

"What's the matter with you?" Oliver asked.

"Let me count the ways," Glen said.

"Please don't," Oliver begged as the officers got out of their respective vehicles.

Glen bit his tongue when Vince Warner glared at him. "Well, long time no see Glen."

"Not long enough, Warden," Glen told the fish and game officer.

"What've we got here, gentlemen?" Sheriff Eugene Winslow asked.

"Eli here tripped on sumthin' when going out to go fishing," Glen explained.

"Your foot?" Vince was acting suspicious when, in reality, he was just busting Glen's saggy balls.

To everyone's shock, he didn't respond to that. Instead, he stepped out of the way of a half-eaten body.

"Is that Samuel Powers?" Sheriff Eugene asked.

"What's left of him," Stan said coldly.

"Jesus, she's making her way up this river now. No doubt about it. She'll probably be in the ocean by later this morning," Sheriff Eugene Winslow explained.

"If she's heading that way, it could even be in the next half hour," Glen began. "But, there ain't no need to jump to conclusions. Sheriff, you and your deputy boy better go patrol the ocean. We've got the everglades."

"We haven't seen one damn scale and already this hermit is giving us orders?!" Vince Warner snapped.

"I trust him and all the overwhelming evidence suggesting that it is a crocodile. I also don't want any problems between you and Mr. Porter here. We need to work together to take this animal down." Sheriff Eugene Winslow took a long winded breath after that speech.

"You have no authority over me," Vince Warner chuckled.

"I can supersede all over your snide ass." The sheriff smiled as he turned to face the game warden.

Sheriff Eugene Winslow could barely see his reflection in Vince Warner's sunglasses. "You might want to clean your glasses too. It might affect your aim."

The sheriff then walked back to his cruiser, got in and began to drive off. He stopped next to Vince and the others.

"Eli, go home. The rest of you, find this abomination against nature. I'll call the coroner to come and pick up Samuel."

He then drove away. Vince could see that he was on his radio already fulfilling his part of the plan. "Alright, men," he shouted, turning to the three hunters. Eli was already on his way back to his blue pick-up truck. "We'll use my boat. My number one rule is to not make any messes when aboard. That includes chewing tobacco." He locked eyes with Stan who spit out some.

"Don't worry; it's the last of my stash anyway," he lied.

The four men then waited for the coroner to arrive.

When he did about fifteen minutes later, he had a look of anger about him. "This is a crime scene, no?"

"Yeah, I guess so," Vince said.

"You're just lucky no one was around. This place should've been secured with caution tape and at least one guard."

"I guess the sheriff's just got bigger things to worry about," Glen said.

"Yeah, I bet," the coroner said as he walked over and began to examine the body. Vince knew this'd take a while but didn't want to speak up. He was already embarrassed and it was all the sheriff's fault.

It wasn't until the ambulance pulled up that Vince felt comfortable leaving. He asked if the coroner was all set and he waved him off. The four men then piled into the fish and game cruiser, a big tan truck with siren lights atop it, and drove towards the docks.

When they arrived, Vince felt there was something off about the scene. Then it dawned on him. "Shit! The tree huggers! They've already gone out!"

"Well then, we'll have to keep an eye out for them as well as the crocodile." Glen smirked towards Vince and then climbed aboard the patrol boat.

"Permission granted, I guess," Vince said.

Stan and Oliver looked at each other. They knew this was going to be a long trip.

CHAPTER ELEVEN

It was a bad idea.

Detouring away from their planned destination, the group decided to visit the cove. It was mainly Kyle's idea, suggesting that the nets might have something worth noting and that it couldn't hurt just to check them out. To his surprise, everyone not only agreed, but they seemed genuinely interested.

Still, Kyle couldn't help but think this was a bad idea. The nagging feeling caused the hairs on his neck to stand up. It was as if he had been brushed by death's hand in one foul swoop. He had the feeling that this was the worst decision of his life. However, his intrigue in what could be in those nets won him over.

They'd be in and out. He reassured himself over and over again all the way until they were at the cove's entrance. It was still as magnificent as ever. Their netting still remained on the left side facing towards the island. The willows nearby hung especially low today. It was like they were covering something up.

Kyle was beginning to have a small panic attack. A sudden rush of dread that only intensified once the hull of the boat slid onto the sand.

Tiffany and Lola hopped off first. Mitch and Dallas were still collecting supplies when Kyle heard the surge of water from behind. It made a whooshing sound that Dallas seemed to notice too as he and Kyle turned to look behind them.

Instinctively, Dallas shoved Mitch off the boat and onto the sandy ground below.

"What the hell, man?!" Mitch shouted as he grasped his knee.

Lola and Tiffany rushed to his aid; all the while the boat began to slide back into the lagoon. Dallas turned back to see that a huge pair of jaws had bitten into the fan. The blades shattered under the dinosaur-like teeth. Kyle could only stare and watch.

Soon, the boat was in the middle of the cove. It was almost right between the entrance and the atoll. The crocodile had let go. The water frothed and rippled as the reptile submerged into the murky depths.

The two men just stood there for a few moments. They were shook to their very core. Dallas had done bull riding before and managed to hold on. Once even for a couple of minutes. However, there was something about slowly being dragged out into the water by some aquatic predator that scared Dallas more than any stupid cow.

Kyle then jumped in the driver's seat and put the boat into full throttle. However, it didn't cooperate.

"Dallas, see if you can fix it!"

"I ain't goin' over there, man!"

"Okay, then I guess we can swim back!" Kyle said with a crazed look in his eye.

Dallas didn't like the sound of that idea at all and carefully made his way over towards the back of the fan boat. Instantly upon inspection, he noticed that some of the fans were warped and one was almost dislodged from the others. It was practically hanging on.

The two men could hear the others shouting from the atoll. Dallas turned to look at Lola. She was quite the fetching woman even when in total fear. For a brief instant, Dallas thought of their time together last night. He wished he were in her arms again. Embracing, tenderness, and eventually satisfaction with each other, he gave their relationship the summer. If it didn't work out, he'd end it.

Instead of that plan, their relationship ended in two seconds... as did Dallas' life.

Grabbed by the head, Dallas Jacobson was yanked from the boat and dragged into the water. Lola screamed so loud that Kyle stopped what he was doing and turned to see what his good buddy was up to. However, he wasn't there.

Kyle peered over the side and saw blood rushing to the surface. He often wondered if it would be like that of B-grade movies. Where the blood doesn't move around but is instead pumped in one spot to the surface. He always laughed at that.

He wasn't laughing now. Instead, he quickly analyzed what was happening. Dallas was being torn apart or worse, in a death roll. A way of dying that was confirmed when some of the crocodile's black scale-laden body turned over and shined on the surface.

"Oh my god, oh my god!" Kyle didn't know what do to.

"Swim, man!" It was Mitch who screamed the command.

To his credit, Kyle didn't hesitate. Instead of panicking, he got off the driver's chair, ran and dived over the edge of the fan boat.

To the group on shore's amazement, the crocodile smashed into the vessel and toppled over it. The jaws of the reptilian behemoth snapped and its head swung to and fro. Eventually, it fell off and back into the swampy water.

That was when Kyle surfaced. He didn't bother looking back at the fan boat for he heard the crash and knew it wasn't there anyway. Hand over head, one at a time, he sped to shore. Adrenaline drove him faster than he ever thought he could swim.

Lola was sobbing further from the shore near a tree. She couldn't see another one of her friends die. Not after Dallas, whom she cared so deeply for. Tiffany and Mitch were already entering the water ready to help Kyle when he made it.

If only he had.

He was suddenly sucked under the water. Mitch screamed obscenities while Tiffany stood there shocked. Kyle Felton never resurfaced. In his place, the water turned a dark crimson.

"Shit!" Mitch finished off his cursing fit.

"What do we do?!" Lola screamed.

"I don't know!" Mitch shouted.

Tiffany continued to stare out towards where Dallas, Kyle and the fan boat used to be.

"We won't survive at night. This whole island will be underwater!" Lola said between sobs.

"It doesn't matter. Crocodiles can come on land! We're screwed no matter what!" Mitch explained.

Tiffany remained motionless. Mitch noticed and began to make his way back into the shallows. He had to comfort her. Lola was beyond gone, she was freaked out. Tiffany was too perhaps but at least she wasn't losing her cool.

And then she was gone.

She was there one second, a few feet away, and then gone the next.

"Tiffany..?" Mitch asked quietly.

"Oh no…" Lola whined quietly to herself.

"Tiffany!" Mitch shouted this time.

There was no response. Not even a ripple on the water. She had disappeared, except this time there was no blood on the surface.

***

Two meaty morsels lay on the bottom of her domain; the third was currently being swallowed whole. She hadn't even attempted to do so; the prey just flowed down her gullet with the rush of water that flowed into her mouth. Similar to a chunky cookie being washed down with milk.

She was satisfied for now. The need to fill her stomach would be subdued for the time being. If necessary, she'd feast on the corpses below. She had already lost one and did not plan to lose anymore.

The crocodile decided to venture out. Not just out of her domain, but the everglades in general. There had to be more of a food source further up north. Given the distance and speed she'd swim, she'd burn enough calories to warrant consuming more. She would return with a bountiful.

Approaching the saltier water, the crocodile swam below a bridge. There was a man on it. He was making his way across.

However, the ancient animal decided to continue on. She could only hold so much in her nine-foot jaw span.

Several miles later, the current rushed past her and she entered a different environment unlike anything she had experienced before. The algae was different, it sat on rocks in abundance instead of resting on the surface. The water was much clearer than her home's. Even with the nictitating lens that spread across her retina, she could tell by the blue hues compared to the green ones from before.

***

Eli Weber had seen enough to know not to go into the water today. Settling on a bridge that overlooked the river, he cast his rod and placed his elbows on the wooden frame. This was the kind of life he enjoyed. No matter what was going on in the water, there was always somewhere else he could go.

As he peered over the edge, hoping to see a catfish or something near his line, his jaw dropped. The gargantuan girth of the crocodile was what took him by surprise first. This was followed by the length. The crocodile must've been around forty feet.

In utter awe, he dropped his fishing net. He didn't even attempt to catch it. As the animal made its way under the bridge, he could see that it was looking at him as if contemplating on whether to attack or not. Eli gripped the siding of the bridge as his knuckles turned white.

As the crocodile passed under, it didn't bother turning back to attack. The bridge was only five or six feet off the ground and twenty feet across. It could've easily taken him out. Apparently it opted to venture out further.

Eli decided then and there that he had to warn somebody. Anybody that would listen would do. That's when he decided to seek out Glen. It was also the time he metaphorically kicked himself in the butt for never getting a cellphone.

***

Tanner decided to head back to the hotel. He knew what time it was but wondered if the group had left without him. He tried to call Kyle but there was no answer. When he got to the hotel and knocked on both doors to their respective rooms, he realized they had gone out already.

He went to the van and decided to try out by the docks. Tanner was beginning to get worried. It wasn't like them not to call. He had talked to Kyle last night. Maybe he just assumed. It was a possibility.

When he got to the docks he saw that the fan boat was gone. He cursed under his breath and then picked up his cellphone again. He tried to call Dallas first but no response. *What the hell is going on?* he wondered as he dialed Mitch's number next.

There was an answer this time.

"Holy shit, Tanner! I was just about to call you," Mitch said.

"What's going on?"

"We went out to the cove to see if there was anything in the nets. The crocodile, man. It attacked us."

"Is everyone alright; did anyone get hurt?"

There was no response right away, just some scratchy static.

"Me and Lola are alright."

"What about everyone else?"

"Just get out here, man. I just phoned the police. They're sending out a hunting party to come get us."

"How's my brother doing, Dallas, Tiffany?"

"I'd rather not tell you over the phone, man."

Tanner's face turned from an irritated red to a shocked white almost instantly.

"I'll find a way to get out there," Tanner said coldly.

"I'm sorry," Mitch whispered.

Tanner wanted to say that it was alright but, truthfully, nothing was alright. He just said his goodbye and then looked up the mayor's number. It rang a few times longer than he would've liked. Finally, Emma picked up the phone.

"Hello, this is Mayor Darwin speaking."

"Emma I need a boat."

"Tanner?"

"Yes, the crocodile. It just attacked my friends in the cove we visited. I need to get out there."

"I'm sorry," she said empathetically. *"I'll get the sheriff on the line. Maybe he can spare some deputies to assist you."*

"Okay. Have them meet me at the docks. Slip number nine is where we were stationed. That's where I'll be."

"Okay," she said softly. *"Is there anything else you need?"*

"No," Tanner said coldly.

"Alright, I hope everyone's safe out there."

"No, they are not." Tanner was stoic at this point.

"If you need anything, don't hesitate. Call me right away."

"I will, and Emma…"

"Yes?"

"Thank you," Tanner said as he hung up the phone.

***

It took Sheriff Eugene Winslow and Deputy Frank Gaston all of twenty minutes to pull to the docks. Tanner approached them as they entered slip-9. He couldn't help but feel that the patrol boat was symbolic of his friends parking there on many occasions after a hard day's work.

"We have confirmation that the crocodile is heading towards the ocean," Sheriff Eugene Winslow explained. "I think we should head out to the cove and let the hunters take care of the animal. Your friends might be out there a little longer but the sooner we can bag this thing, the better."

"Agreed," Tanner said as he climbed into the boat and got seated in the chair next to the dashboard.

They drove off as Sheriff Eugene Winslow radioed Vince to tell the hunters to come back and go hunt the crocodile.

"What about the kids, over?" Vince asked.

"We're heading out there to get them now. Just haul ass. If Eli warned you an hour ago, that creature could have caused who knows what kind of damage in that time. We need to minimalize the damage and take care of the threat, over."

"Understood, over," Vince said over the radio.

"Let's take care of this problem once and for all. Over and out." Sheriff Eugene Winslow placed the receiver back onto the clip.

***

Mitch and Lola were sitting tight in the middle of the atoll. They both wanted to say something whether it be reassurance or some kind of good gesture to their lost friends. However, neither of them wanted to speak in fear of the crocodile or some other animal hearing them and they definitely didn't want to go anywhere near the water to pay their respects.

There was a swooshing of water off to the right on Lola's side that made her jump. Mitch held her and she buried her head in his chest. The act comforted both of them.

"I hope they get here soon," Lola finally spoke.

"Me too," Mitch said quietly.

Suddenly, there was a splash right next to Lola. She began to freak out and head for the water. Mitch turned to see what was scaring her and saw that it was a snake - an anaconda to be precise.

The great twenty-foot serpent slithered towards Mitch as he followed Lola into the water. They both knew it was a death sentence but being swiftly killed by a crocodile or slowly constricted by a snake made them choose the latter. Both were horrible ways to die though.

Swimming straight for an opening that led into a patch of land, they hastened their pace. They didn't bother looking back. They could hear the snake hissing behind them.

Lola managed to get ashore first and she grabbed Mitch's arm. She pulled and pulled but only managed in making him uncomfortable. Soon, he was halfway on the mushy ground. He figured there wasn't much time left so he fought the earth below and managed to somehow slide his way to the top. He collapsed onto Lola in the mud. Mitch looked at her. He never realized how drop dead gorgeous she was before. Maybe he was too focused on Tiffany.

Hissssssss.

The two looked back the way they came fully expecting to see the snake. However, it wasn't on shore. It wasn't even in the water but, instead, still on the atoll. The constrictor began to coil around a certain spot.

"We must've been near her nest," Mitch explained.

"How come we never saw it?" Lola asked.

"We weren't necessarily hanging around in the bushes on the atoll before, ya know," Mitch said matter-of-factly.

Lola began to sob. "What if they drive by and don't see us on the atoll anymore? What if they assume we're already dead?!"

"I'm sure they'll come investigate. As long as we stay where we are now, they can find us."

"Okay." She half-smiled.

Mitch put a finger under her chin. "Don't worry, I'm not going to let anything happen to you."

She fully smiled at that. "I know."

The two stood there and waited for their rescue party to come. They would've been content being there hours had they not heard another splash.

"What now?" Lola asked.

Suddenly, as if to answer, an alligator emerged from the water and, unlike Mitch, found it very easy to scale the slippery steep hill. It was soon right in front of them.

"What is with this cove today?" Mitch said, annoyed. "When the crocodile leaves do all the other critters come out to play?"

"Run, damnit!" Lola screamed at him.

Mitch couldn't get his legs to work right away but managed to bend his knee slightly and then begin jogging. That jog turned into a sprint alongside Lola. Soon, when Mitch looked over his shoulder, the atoll was out-of-sight.

CHAPTER TWELVE

It was a home away from home

Joel Kinnear loved to take business trips to Florida. He'd spend most of his time on the coast doing his daily activities. He'd jog in the morning and afternoon and sunbathe in-between. At night he'd hit the local clubs and drink to himself. He appreciated any company that came his way. He was glad he never married; less risk involved.

That was the thing about Joel Kinnear, he was a strategist. He didn't take risks unless there was a good chance of success. As a man of the big business corporation that worked on making sunglasses for the hard-of-seeing, he was a revolutionist. Usually, you had to wear clip on ones or buy a prescribed pair. With ideas always floating around in his head, he was preparing to make regular glasses that could convert to fight off the shade just by the rays of intense light. It'd beat the middle-man of having to put on the extra accessory. It was, in a sense, the ultimate pair of glasses. Others complained that it wasn't original and wouldn't fund the project. Joel figured he wouldn't need them and that, even if it wasn't wholly original, the advertisements would lure people in.

Putting his arms over his head, Joel stretched. He was preparing for another afternoon jog. It was only a little after eleven but it was close enough to mid-day that he decided to go ahead and take a nice stroll down the white sandy beach. Maybe if he felt up to it he'd go again later.

Unfortunately, his routine swim was out of the question as the beaches were closed from the water out. There weren't many people on the beach at this time. In fact, it looked like it was just a mother and her two kids. Joel did a quick jog in place and then was off.

Creativity was one of Joel's other strong characteristics. He was an innovator and usually got his ideas either when he was in the shower or on the beach. In this case though, his mind seemed absent today for some reason. His attention was focused on the water. He kept trying to avert his eyes from it but something seemed off about it. At first he figured it was because the water was empty.

Soon, he was by the mother and her two children. Joel almost didn't notice for his mind was focused elsewhere – the mother was drop dead gorgeous. What's more is that she didn't have a ring on her finger which was evident by her holding a paperback of some bigfoot book with the monster on the front, a car upturned and a sign that read Cauldron Creek.

Her kids were playing in the sand as he jogged by. However, after he did so, they dropped their buckets and shovels used to play in the sand and charged for the water. The mother didn't notice at first but, as she turned the page, she saw that her children were gone. Sitting up, she called for them. Joel heard the names *Kris* and *Valarie* and he turned around to see what was wrong.

Kris outpaced his sister and entered the water first. Valarie was not far behind. They began to splash and try to cool off from the muggy Floridian air. The water wasn't particularly cold but it was refreshing nevertheless. They did hear their mother calling but were too preoccupied to notice the angered tone in her voice.

Joel had seen it first. A massive black shape appeared in the water and darted for the two kids. It was gargantuan and, at first, he thought it was one of those prehistoric sharks. He then looked to the mother who seemed to have noticed it too, for her face was pale.

His strategic pattern played out in his mind. He could try to save those kids and possibly die. Or he could succeed and maybe get a little something out of it. She'd be a lot better than talking to the drunk at the club *again* tonight. For once, he chose to go against his gut feeling that it was a bad idea. Before he knew it, he was running for the water. His legs took over while his mind pondered on what to do.

Valarie felt something was off. The man who ran by before was now running for them. He entered the water with great haste, kicking it up as he marched forward. Droplets were flying around him and then he dived.

Kris hadn't realized how far they were out. It was thirty, maybe thirty-five yards. He too noticed the man but only right as he dived. He looked to his mother who appeared as though she were going to faint. Something was very wrong.

Joel suddenly surfaced and began swimming like a professional athlete in the aquatic sports department. His adrenaline kept his speed up and he wasn't showing any signs of slowing. Soon, he was upon the kids and tried to grab them. However, their arms were slippery. Add to that the fact that they weren't going with him without a fight.

"There's no time!" Joel screamed.

"Are you crazy?!" Valarie shouted.

Joel looked to the right of the kids. The dark figure was now fifty yards away. This clued Valarie and Kris that there was something out there and, for the second time, they acknowledged their whereabouts.

"Let's go!" Joel shouted at them.

This time there was no protest. Kris and Valarie were shoved in front of the man and they swam. Joel would cover them for as long as he could.

Deep down, he couldn't seem to forgive himself. This was a stupid idea. It'd never work. The risk was too great. They'd all die. As he thought this, he never let it overcome him. He still remained behind the kids to watch over them.

When five yards remained between them and the sandy beach, the mother screamed. Joel chanced a glance over his shoulder and his eyes nearly bulged out of their sockets.

It wasn't a shark.

The black scale-laden beast with the piercing eyes with diamond pupils was taking its time behind them. It couldn't have been more than a few inches from Joel's feet. He wanted to push past the kids and swim for his life but something within him kept him going the same pace.

Valarie reached the beach first followed by Kris. The mother hugged her kids and then quickly ran to help Joel. He was on the beach now but so was the crocodile. A deep guttural growl emitted from the reptile as it approached.

Joel grabbed the umbrella that had been there to provide shade for the kids. He began to make jabbing motions with it at the crocodile. It didn't seem impressed.

"Run!" Joel screamed over his shoulder.

The mother and her two children began to back away slowly.

"Run!" Joel screamed again.

That seemed to do the trick as it snapped the mother out of her trance-like state and she began to run with her two kids towards the parking lot.

Deciding to cut his losses, Joel javelined the closed umbrella at the crocodile and then took off. When he was at the parking lot, he dared a look back. The crocodile was gone. It obviously entered the water but there was barely even a ripple on the surface.

He turned and saw the mother standing there with her two kids. "Are you alright?"

They all nodded.

Then the mother walked up to Joel and began to shower him with kisses. Her kids looked away in disgust. Joel took her in his arms as their lips parted.

"Dinner, my place?"

"You've got it. My name's Kim."

"Nice to meet you, Kim."

He gave her directions to his place and then she walked away with her children close by. Joel couldn't help but ogle at her figure. She had a nice rump. He then turned and walked back to his room at the motel. The whole time, he was grateful that this time the stupid risk paid off.

***

She had returned to the sea. It was a natural instinct for safety. There was no need to travel far inland when there were an abundance of other sounds out in the ocean that'd lead to prey. It wasn't slim pickings like it was back in the everglades.

With the lens covering her eyes, her nostrils acted as her sight, picking up signs of prey in distress or just nearby. She could smell blood everywhere whether it were nearby or a mile away. That wasn't even the extent of her nasal capabilities. They could easy smell further out. However, it was at that mile-mark that she sensed water chemicals. They were being released by what was presumably rotted flesh.

Her senses heightened, she began to sway her tail back and forth. She was practically slithering through the water now. Her smell acted as metaphorical binoculars as it guided her towards her target.

Hovering a few feet from the surface, her black scale-laden body could still feel the heat of the sun bearing down on her. This time though, the water was cooler and more refreshing than the mugginess of the everglades. In the back of her ancient mind, she decided it'd not only be preferable to stay at this depth, but safer. Whatever was emitting the smell had been dead for a while and was recently dropped into the sea.

There had been plenty of traps in the past that she had been entangled in. Surviving each encounter, she took away from it lessons that could be attributed later. In this instance, it was a type of trap that she was all too familiar with.

***

Glen Porter sat on the boat, his hand shining with blood from dropping the bait overboard. Oliver was working on a lure with hooks sticking out of it. As far as Stan was concerned, he was the sharp shooter on this little skirmish.

The plan entailed the lure to be consumed by the crocodile. The hooks would sink into its tender flesh inside its mouth and, as it tried to make its escape, Glen would activate the dynamite attached to the lure and set off a massive explosion, finally ridding the world of the killer crocodile.

For good measure, a raccoon that Glen had found on the way to the docks had been gutted and attached to one of the long hooks. Now all that was left to do was chum the water. Glen also decided to dunk his arm up to his elbow in the fish guts and toss them out for good measure.

"I hope there aren't any sharks that come by," Stan said apprehensively. He didn't want to be picked on.

"No need for cowardliness," Glen explained. "No shark will want to be around by the time the beast comes our way."

"Good point," Stan said ashamedly.

Suddenly, there was a splash followed by a surge of water pushing past a black mass. Stan stood in his place, frozen with fear. Oliver didn't fare much better. Glen took his hand out of the innards and looked on at the great beast.

"There she is, boys."

Oliver was a bit taken aback. For the longest time, he thought Glen just made everything up. However, seeing this killer crocodile before him was enough to make him a believer in whatever Glen would spew out next.

"She's real..." Stan said what Oliver was thinking.

"Damn right she is and she's coming this way," Glen stated.

Stan instinctively raised the rifle at the mass and fired. The bullet bounced off her hide.

"Damnit, man! Wait until you can either get an eye or underbelly shot. Otherwise, you're just wasting bullets!" Glen shouted.

The croc was now charging for the little boat. Glen began to think that they should've invested in something bigger. Suddenly, she took a wide turn which caused the boat to rock from the incoming wavelets.

"She's going for the bait, boys!" Glen was giddy with anticipation.

At that moment, Vince Warner shot up from the driver's chair. He had passed out but began to get queasy when the boat was swaying. He looked down at the three idiots who were looking out at something.

Holy shit.

He couldn't believe it. It was a gargantuan black crocodile; just as Glen described. The dark scale-laden body was covered in seaweed and barnacles. The creature was old, ancient, a relic from the time of the dinosaurs.

Ten years in the fish and game department and he never felt such admiration for an animal before. She was literally the perfect specimen. He looked down on the deck and just then noticed all the gear.

I can't let them kill it! Vince thought. It was their sole mission for being out there. It had claimed several lives and would take more if not stopped. Part of him wanted to just capture it. However, Glen would never go for that idea. The creature had killed his friend.

The crocodile was now making her way towards a contraption of sorts. Vince realized that it was no doubt an explosive lure. She'd be done for. He had to do something. This creature had to be protected.

To his left there was a small tool box. He rushed to it and opened it to look through its contents. There was a screwdriver, some flares with a flare gun, a small hammer and a round object. It was black and bumpy like the crocodile's scales. The small circular item was a grenade.

Standing up straight, he unclipped the pin, brought it over his shoulder, took aim, and threw the explosive. A few seconds passed after it hit the water ten feet from the crocodile.

Boom!

Glen, Stan, and Oliver all crouched down. Glen had done so before the grenade even went off. Stan and Oliver were just lucky they had good reflexes.

"What the hell's the matter with ya?!" Glen shouted back towards the center console.

"Did you see that thing? It's practically a damn dinosaur!" Vince tried to use shock with reason to make his case.

"Yeah, and that prehistoric prick will get away and probably kill more people now. All thanks to you!" Glen was screaming now.

Vince didn't reply. Instead, he slunk back into his captain's chair and took in what he just saw. It was astonishing that such a creature existed in this day and age. It made him wonder what else the everglades could be hiding.

Deep down though, he had a feeling he knew exactly what caused this unnatural oddity.

***

They were cold and on edge. Mitch was sitting uncomfortably on the flattest rock he could find. It was large enough to fit two people, hence why Lola sat next to him. It was cold and made their bums sore, but it was enough.

After all they had been through, Mitch had just now realized how little he had actually talked to Lola. He couldn't figure out why. She was a beautiful woman with a great mind and an exotic accent. While she may have been a bit testy, it was always warranted. He felt bad for her though, for he knew that she had a thing for Dallas.

Lola felt similar but almost worse for Mitch. She and Dallas never even made it to first base while Mitch and Tiffany were practically a couple. Now, Dallas and Tiffany, as well as Kyle, were all dead and they were left stuck in a mud patch.

Surrounded on all sides by water, the forestry of this particular part of the everglades didn't lead to solid land. Every step resulted in a squelching sound as their boots sunk in and then pulled out ending with a suction-like noise.

They were both amazed they even found a rock at all. Much like the atoll, this area wouldn't be above water level for much longer. In fact, since they arrived, the tide had risen up to a few inches below the top of the rock. The pair didn't dare look into the murky blackness below them. Not only did it resemble tar or oil but it looked like the shading of the killer crocodile herself.

Both of them had remained silent for what seemed like an eternity, when in reality it had only been an hour. They were busy keeping an ear out for the sound of a boat or chopper or any motorized vehicle that could rescue them.

However, that feeling of hope was dwindling fast.

Mitch was sure he'd be the first to crack. Make a noise or talk, either way he figured he'd annoy Lola. So it came as a total surprise when she cleared her throat. He looked at her instantly.

"Thank you for not leaving me."

"Why would I do that?"

"Most guys would've."

"Not true but I'll still take the compliment."

"Well, every guy I've gone out with would have," Lola sighed.

"Then you've been dating the wrong kind of guys."

There was a drawn out pause.

"I wish I knew if Dallas was different than them," Lola said finally.

"Listen. We can't reflect on the past right now. We need to focus on the here and now to survive. There'll be time for grieving later."

Mitch thought she'd argue with him but she shocked him again by nodding.

"Whatever happens I won't leave you. I'll keep you safe and we'll make it out of here. You'll see." Mitch gave her a warm smile.

"I believe you," Lola said as she snuggled into his chest.

Despite her being caked in dried mud and having a mess of hair, she still looked gorgeous. Mitch decided to focus on the water below them. He promised himself that he wouldn't but he needed to focus.

Just then, there was a low droning sound. It began to get louder, more guttural. Mitch and Lola both sat up realizing what it was simultaneously. It was an engine.

"We're going to have to get in the water," Mitch said gravely.

"What?! Are you crazy?"

"No, in fact, you stay here and I'll go get them and I'll come back for you."

Lola thought it over for a few seconds. "I'm not letting you go alone."

"There's no time to argue!"

"If you don't make it and I don't know that you didn't, then how will I be able to get their attention?"

"What?" Mitch was barely focusing on her words, instead trying to see past the foliage.

"By the time they leave, I'll probably have found out that you didn't survive. I'll be stuck out here alone."

That got Mitch's attention.

"Alright, let's go. But be as quiet as possible," Mitch said.

He gave a slow countdown from three to one with his fingers and then they both placed their feet in the water together. Soon, they slid off the rock and were nearly waist deep. Their feet didn't stick in the mud as much as before but it was still hard to walk. They pressed on though.

Soon, they could hear the engine cut out. Tanner called out for them.

"We're here!" Lola screamed.

She began to run forward as best she could. Mitch tried to grab for her but she slipped away. He decided not to scream to get her back over here and instead to use that energy to chase her down.

Lola couldn't believe it. This nightmare was going to be over and she could return to the motel. She couldn't wait to get back on an airplane and take her one-way ticket back to Australia. It wasn't the most comforting of feelings given that that continent's animal kingdom would put this one to shame. However, she was in the thick of it and she'd rather be back in her own room. It had a hammock, light blue wallpaper, a wind chime that'd blow softly in the wind, a window to look out of, a carpeted floor that felt good on her feet as opposed to this stinky mud; a poster of the animal kingdom was on her wall too. It featured snakes, kangaroos, spiders, scorpions, crocodiles…

Splash!

It appeared right in front of her. The ten foot reptile erupted from the murky bottom and snapped right at Lola. She fell back right before the maw closed on her pretty little head. Mitch was close behind. He managed to get ahold of her this time and pick her up out of the swampy water.

The alligator had been waiting for them this whole time.

"What do we do?" Lola squealed.

"Tanner!" Mitch shouted.

"Tanner, we're back here! Please help us!" Lola cried out.

Mitch began to guide Lola backwards away from the encroaching alligator. It was slowly gliding towards them. Its legs weren't even visible below the murk as though it were just a flat mass floating over.

The two closed their eyes hoping for a quick death. However, Lola and especially Mitch knew it wouldn't be given how these beasts operate. It'd tenderize them, leave them to bloat and then consume them. They'd be dead and lying in an underwater hole somewhere, waiting to be eaten and digested properly.

Bang.

A squirt of blood hit Lola on the face. It was a small amount compared to the spray that erupted from the alligator's eye. It let out an agonized hissing sound and then rolled over dead.

Taking a few seconds to open their eyes, Mitch and Lola were greeted by the sight of Tanner. With him were the sheriff and a deputy.

"Oh thank god!" Mitch sighed with relief.

"Let's get you kids out of here," Sheriff Eugene Winslow said as he helped them aboard the patrol boat.

Tanner looked around for Kyle, Dallas, and Tiffany. Mitch turned around to see him scanning the waters. He put a hand on his friend's shoulder.

"I'm sorry, Tan. They're gone."

Tanner didn't even bother sitting in a chair. He just fell into the hull and placed his hands on his face. Lola and Mitch sat on opposite sides of him and joined in on the sobbing.

CHAPTER THIRTEEN

It was a bad idea.

Sadie Stone was sick to death of her boyfriend's wild ideas. They always ended in embarrassment for her. With the coming of her eighteenth birthday, she wanted to give herself to Patrick but every chance she advanced on him, he had a new cockamamie idea. Last week, it was riding down in the everglades with a canoe that he equipped with a motor. The whole premise not only looked stupid but defeated the purpose of canoeing.

This week was a new low for Patrick Forester though. He decided to go windsurfing with her. However, the sail-board-thing, whatever it was, wasn't going to hold her, she thought. Knowing this, she asked what his new idea was that he brainstormed (or brain farted). She vaguely recalled him holding out his hands to her as if he were performing a magic trick.

"I'll tow you along on a surfboard!"

She laughed at him.

"No, seriously! It'll be fun, Sadie. Plus, I've got both boards looking smooth."

"About as smooth as that pick-up line you gave to that girl at the bar last week."

"That wasn't a pick-up line, Sadie! I was just being nice."

"Oh, sure... you saying 'Bikinis are overrated" wasn't you just trying to say that you're only interested in her body."

"No, I just prefer the natural look of a woman undressed." Patrick smirked.

"You just made it worse," Sadie said coldly.

There was a drawn out pause between the two that lasted until early dawn.

Sadie gave in and decided to take Patrick up on his stupid escapade. He beamed with a face that shone like the coming sun. By the time they reached the shoreline of Sadie's parent's beach house, Patrick was already jittering with excitement. He kicked off his sandals and proceeded to tie a knot between the two boards. Next, he and Sadie walked out into the shallows and soon they were up to their chests.

Climbing atop the smooth board, she had to admit that it did feel nice and that Patrick had done a good job cleaning it. She looked up at her boyfriend and noticed how attractive he was as he easily hopped up and sat atop his windsurf board.

Soon they were off.

Sadie watched Patrick glide across the slight chop of the ocean. The water did eventually level out and become more flat. That was when she noticed that the wind was picking up. It was really a perfect day for this particular activity.

Eventually, Sadie's thoughts went to her birthday. It was a week away and she was so eager to get in Patrick's pants. She didn't want anything else from him. The celebration of their bodies pressed against each other was good enough for her. It'd be the best present in the world. He'd caress her breasts and then between her thighs. She'd make him feel good.

The location was simple. She chose a small patch of brush that she liked to hang out at when she was a kid. It wasn't too far from the house and it had a semimetal value. *God I love how he looks on that thing.* Sadie smiled.

As for herself, Sadie Stone was now the popular high school cheerleader sitting on a board while her boyfriend sailed for her. For once, she didn't care if she looked ridiculous. This was fun, this was life, this was love.

She couldn't take her eyes off of Patrick. Not even when his windsurf board exploded out of the water. Her expression changed from admiration to horror, but her eyes never left him. He was thrown into the air with splintered pieces of wood all around him. He looked like a rag doll being flung into the air. As he fell back to the earth, a pair of tooth laden jaws opened up. He disappeared down the gullet of the hideous scaly monster.

Putting her hands over her head, Sadie Stone wanted the thing to disappear. However, she heard the sound of an encroaching swell. Her time was coming up. There was no escape for her. This is it; this is how she'd die. Her demise would be on the smooth board that made her look ridiculous.

"Patrick!" she screamed, knowing full well he was gone.

Just then, a pair of arms grabbed her and hauled her onto a boat. Sadie tried to focus as the sounds of shots being fired made her feel lightheaded. She looked up to see three men firing at the creature. There was a fourth one with a pair of sunglasses that was holding her. He was kind of cute; too old for her, but still cute.

"I'm out!" the three men seemed to say in unison.

The one holding her sat her in a chair and then ran away. She reached out for him but all she felt was empty space. Suddenly, the engine roared to life and they began to go fast. Her curly hair whipped around in the wind and tickled her still wet face. She brushed it out of the way only to see the creature. It was following them. *It must be a hundred feet long,* Sadie thought to herself. *No creature in the world should be that big.*

"Get to shore!" the older man of the group shouted at a skier and her chauffeur on the boat.

The woman on the ski and man driving reminded her of her predicament. She was older but much prettier than Sadie. No animal, man or beast, should take that beautiful woman with the hunk for a husband away from each other.

"Crocodile!" Sadie screamed, surprised that she even remembered what a crocodile was. Was there even a difference between a crocodile and alligator?

There were more pressing matters at hand.

The crocodile had now changed direction and was heading for the skier. The man swerved left and right trying to protect the woman whom was nearly falling off at every turn. She looked annoyed. *She hasn't seen it yet,* Sadie thought to herself.

Finally, after what seemed like hours, when in reality it was only thirty seconds, the crocodile submerged into the ocean blue.

It wasn't for long.

The same pair of jaws that engulfed Patrick exploded from the water right below the skier. She was screaming at her husband, unaware that the dark cavernous void was consuming her from below. She didn't even get a chance to scream.

The man grabbed out what appeared to be a big knife. He then dived overboard to rescue his woman.

Sadie covered her mouth with her hands. This was becoming too much. The thought of seeing another person killed made her feel ill. She looked around for a bucket and saw one. She picked it up and was about to puke when she noticed it was filled with blood and fish innards. That was the breaking point and she up-chucked the contents from her breakfast into the chum bucket.

"Thanks for the extra goodies," the older man said over his shoulder.

It then dawned on Sadie that this wasn't right. "What're you guys doing out here anyway?"

"Quiet, girl, I'm trying to concentrate," the youngest of the group said. He was a bum-looking man with crusty straight hair and a tattered tan top hat.

"What's your name?" she asked him.

"Stu," he said quietly.

"Well, Stu. Here's the thing. Don't tell me to be quiet. I don't need a man telling me what to do!"

"Oh boy," Stu chuckled.

Just then, the hunky husband burst from the water. He was out-of-breath. "Where is it?!" he shouted.

"We don't know," the shades-wearing man said. "Glen, do you see anything?" He was referring to the older fellow.

"Not a fuckin' thing. What about you, Oliver?"

A Latino man looked at Glen and simply shook his head.

"I've got to find her!" the hunky husband said.

Before anyone could object, he dove again.

Oliver walked over to the sunglasses man and confronted him face-to-face. "This is getting ridiculous, Vince. Get us out of here."

"Vince," Sadie whispered. "Please do what he says."

"First we have to get that man out of there," Vince said as he walked over towards the edge of the boat.

Bump.

"Port side!" Glen shouted.

Before Sadie realized that she was on the port side, she felt a searing pain in her arm. The crocodile had her now. It dragged her over the side. Spinning round and round, she couldn't scream, couldn't mourn, couldn't even cry from the saltwater stinging her eyes. All she could do was think of the best birthday she'd never get to have.

***

When Vince Warner helped the babbling girl onto the boat, he made it his mission to protect her. He failed almost immediately. The water frothed as she was spun around in a death roll. He ran to the port side and began firing at the crocodile. It didn't really matter if he hit the girl at this point. She was already dead.

Stan and Oliver ran over and joined Vince in the fire show. Glen casually made his way towards them and decided that it wasn't worth his time.

"Stop firing!" he screamed loud enough just for Vince to hear.

"Why?"

"There's no point. She's dead and our guns are useless against that crocodile."

"I don't believe that."

"Then what do you believe, Mr. Warner?"

Vince stopped himself from opening fire again and turned to Glen. "I believe there's a reason this crocodile is so big."

"You don't say."

Vince took a deep breath and began.

"Darwin Institute is…"

A splash formed behind Glen. He turned to see the man who was driving the speedboat. Helping the able bodied man onboard, it was clear he was tired. His chest heaved as he fought to regain composure as well as fill his lungs with air.

"I must have dived twenty feet," he said between breaths. "She's gone."

With that knowledge, the man suddenly stood rigid. His breathing was no longer labored. He then began to sob. "Cassidy, why?"

Glen turned to Vince. "You were saying?"

The two men stared each other down. One having knowledge the other didn't even suspect. Glen was just pushing buttons at this point.

"It's gone!" Stu called over his shoulder.

Vince turned and looked over the side. "Shit!"

"What do we do now?!" Stu asked, his voice wobbly.

No one had an answer for him.

***

Sheriff Eugene Winslow, his deputy, and the three other occupants pulled into the slick. Tanner felt weird getting off the patrol boat after his own boat was destroyed. He wished that his fan boat were still parked there with Kyle, Dallas, and Tiffany sitting there, ready and waiting for their next assignment. Mitch and Lola followed him off.

"You kids pack up your gear and get the hell out of this town. We'll handle this from here on out," Sheriff Eugene Winslow stated.

"If you think I'm going to let that crocodile get away with all this, you're sadly mistaken." Tanner approached the patrol boat.

"Easy there, boy, we don't need any heroes," Deputy Frank Gaston said as he put his hands to his waist.

"Look, we can handle this from here, Tanner. We just need you to cooperate and not get in our way," Sheriff Eugene Winslow said while trying to bring down the tension between his deputy and the conservationist.

It didn't work.

"Listen, you snotty little dweeb," Tanner began. "That thing killed my brother and two of our friends. I'm going out there to stop it. Whether by land or sea, I will be the one to take that croc down."

"Whatever you say," the deputy kept pressing.

"Frank, knock it off!" Sheriff Eugene Winslow snapped.

"No need for formalities, Sheriff. I was just…"

"You were just poking the hornet's nest with a big-fucking-stick!" Sheriff Eugene Winslow finished his deputy's presumed sentence.

"Come on, you two. Let's get out of here," Tanner said as he turned and walked off the dock.

Mitch and Lola followed. They were covered in dirt and their heads hung low. They were a truly pitiful sight but lucky at the same time. They had survived the croc attack.

Sheriff Eugene Winslow and Deputy Frank Gaston pulled out of the slip soon after and made their way out of the everglades and into the conjoining sea.

***

Vince Warner had lost sight of the crocodile. The fish and game warden couldn't even see it on the fish finder. Either the big beast went too deep or she was gone. Shaking his head, he couldn't believe it. The massive animal had disappeared while he argued with Glen. She was there one minute and gone the next.

"This is all your fault," Vince said as he faced Glen.

"My fault?" the grizzled hunter asked. "And, may I inquire, how it is my fault that you didn't keep your eyes on the fish finder?"

There was no response.

Then there was a dull sound. It was similar to a bee buzzing nearby. The five men looked around.

"Over there!" Stan shouted as he pointed out to sea.

"It's the sheriff!" Vince was overjoyed as he walked over to the starboard side of the vessel.

Oliver and Stan joined him while Glen stood looking over the guardrail. Something felt off. It was as if there was a disturbance in the water below.

"What is it?" the hunky husband to the deceased skier asked.

Beep.

Before Glen could turn around all the way, the boat rocked to the right. Oliver, Stan, and Vince all had trouble staying in place while Glen held onto the guardrail for dear life.

There was a surge of water that came over the port side. When the four men turned around, the man they managed to save wasn't there anymore.

"Shit! Where did he go?!" Oliver asked.

"How did something that big get to the surface so fast?" Vince wondered.

"I think you just answered your own question," Glen said.

"What do you mean?" Vince asked.

"Something that big doesn't need that much area to cover. She probably just shot right up from the ocean floor," Glen explained gravely.

Beep.

"She's coming back!" Stan shouted.

Bang!

Shots were fired from the incoming patrol boat. The four men turned to see that the crocodile was charging right for them while Deputy Frank Gaston opened fire. The officer fired until the clip ran empty. He then went to reload.

In all of his years as a police officer, Sheriff Eugene Winslow had never done anything so stupid. However, it was a last minute decision that would inevitably cost him. In one swift motion, he ran the patrol boat over the crocodile's scaly back.

He snapped his head back in the direction of the over-sized reptile to see that not only had he caused no damage to the animal but that his deputy had fallen overboard.

Deputy Frank Gaston surfaced quickly and began to scream for the sheriff. He was thrashing about and creating all sorts of noise. The scene before the sheriff reminded him of his younger brother, Kurt and how they'd pretended to drown one another in the public pools as kids. However, this wasn't the past. This was the present and something had to be done to stop this.

He swung the boat and circled around.

Suddenly, the water below Deputy Frank Gaston began to swirl. It appeared as if it were being drained. The officer didn't quite put two and two together until it was too late.

From below, the thirty-two-foot reptile opened her cavernous jaws. Water rushed in and she had to snap them shut several times. She chomped her way to the surface. Eventually, she found her mark.

Sheriff Eugene Winslow watched in unbelievable horror as his deputy was taken in a surge of saltwater. Inside the great swell was a mighty maw with teeth each the size of his hand. There was a horrible snapping sound almost like two planks of wood being smashed into each other. Then, the blood came both from the deputy's wounds and his mouth. The crocodile had bitten into his midsection. It was all over when the gargantuan beast crashed back into the ocean. The choppy water turned into wavelets. Soon there was barely a ripple on the surface. Then nothing.

The crimson water lapped against the hull of the patrol boat. The deputy was nowhere to be seen. Sheriff Eugene Winslow wondered how he'd tell Frank's sister of his death when suddenly the entire frame of the vessel snapped. Splinters of the deck shot upward and water began to pour in. The single passenger was flung into the air. He barrel rolled mid-flight which resulted in him catapulting into the ocean.

He couldn't get his bearings right away but Sheriff Eugene Winslow managed to maintain a calm demeanor and focused on the rising bubbles. He made his way to the surface in a few seconds and right into the waiting hands of Glen Porter.

The charter boat had pulled up right beside the sheriff right when he hit the water. Vince pinpointed how close to get judging by the sheriff's bubbles and eventually they got him aboard.

"We've got to get out of here," Stu said, shaking. "She's back!"

Oliver and Vince looked out to sea and saw the flat, black-scaled, barnacle-laden back of the beast. Her tail barely even moved yet she was still propelling forward fast. Her red eyes fixated on the boat before her. Nothing would take her attention off the boat.

Vince ran over to the helm and pushed the throttle. As if inched further and further, the boat gained speed. At first, he didn't think it'd be enough. However, as they glided across the water with incredible speed and grace, he was happy with the distance he was putting between them and the crocodile.

However, she never took her eyes off of them.

***

Mitch was the first to see Vince and his boat speeding towards shore. A sudden sense of fear came over him as he noticed the crocodile trailing right behind it. He nudged Tanner on the shoulder and then pointed. Both of them simultaneously felt the gravity of the situation increase when they saw a few kids playing in the shallows.

"Get out of the water!" Lola screamed.

One of the kids turned to her and flipped her off.

Normally, Mitch would've said to forget them and let them get in trouble. It'd hopefully make them see the error of their way. However, now was not the time to start teaching kids a lesson. Not only was a boat charging straight for them, but so was a massive monster.

"Come on, guys!" Mitch shouted.

Surprisingly one of them did listen and got out of the water. She seemed to be getting pressured by her friends to stay but she wasn't having it. *Good for her,* Mitch thought.

"You two as well!" Tanner pointed at the two boys.

Instead of heeding his stern, demanding voice, they began to swim out further.

"Oh my god, I can't watch!" Lola said as her head disappeared into Mitch's shoulder.

***

Emma Darwin was in her limousine on her way to a meeting when she saw Tanner and his two friends on the dock. Part of her wanted to talk with Tanner but the other part of her knew it was a bad idea. She then realized they were shouting at two kids below on the beach.

"Stop the limo," she said hastily.

The driver stopped on a dime and Emma got out. She then ran over to Tanner, Mitch, and Lola. "What's going on?"

Lola looked to her with teary eyes. She then pointed out to sea. It was Vince on a charter boat with three hunters and the sheriff. Emma looked behind them and her pale face turned even whiter.She didn't stop to contemplate on what to do next. She just ran towards the beach.

Tanner wrapped his hands around her before she could get too far. "Stop, we can't help them!"

Boom!

The sound of a gunshot got their attention. Glen held his rifle in the air and then fired another shot. The two boys in the water stopped swimming and looked at the boat as it pulled up beside them. It was massive, comparatively speaking, and dwarfed them.

Stu and Vince helped the two boys aboard. Oliver brushed past the two men and gave the boys a wild look. "Where's Mimi?!"

***

128

Mimi Jones had grown bored of playing with Tommy and Craig. She decided to grab her backpack and head for the docks. *Who needs icky boys anyway?* she thought to herself as she sat on the planks of wood, took off her pack, and removed the doll from inside. It came with a brush that she used on its hair.

She could hear the shouting but didn't pay much attention to it. Soon, she was lost in her own little world. Not even the two gunshots really registered. If anything, she wanted to get a pair of headphones over her ears to block out the noise. Her phone would play music out loud but she always felt embarrassed by what she liked to listen to. Craig would especially make fun of her for it.

However, neither Tommy nor Craig was here right now. She took out her phone, looked through her music list and chose some instrumental jazz song. The world around her disappeared.

***

With a mighty tug, Emma managed to get out of Tanner's grip. It helped that he was focused on the kids getting on the boat. She could hear the sheriff asking where the crocodile went to no one in particular.

It was a few hundred feet but she soon made it to the docks. She felt her breasts weighing her down. She then saw Mimi on the end of the docks dangling her feet off the edge.

"Mimi!" she screamed and then scaled the sand dune that led to pier.

***

The song had ended and Mimi noticed something was off. She turned around to see the mayor lady running straight for her. She had a crazed look on her face that made her shrink back. Managing to right herself before falling over, she was about to get on her feet and try and run around her.

An explosion of water soon sprayed around her little body as a hideous mouth enclosed around her. She disappeared down the crocodile's gullet in one slimy swallow. The reptile then disappeared below the waves.

Emma could only stand there and scream. Her legs wobbled and she soon fell to her knees and began to sob deeply. Tanner found his way by her side and helped her off the dock. The tears turned off and she began to go in shock right as Oliver ran up to her and asked what happened.

CHAPTER FOURTEEN

The sirens blared.

On any other normal day, Emma Darwin would've been annoyed by the sound. However, she found it comforting. It made it apparent that help was on the way. She was being cradled in Tanner's arms as she watched the sea. Glen and Vince were out on the boat again while Stu and Oliver were left on the beach.

Oliver Jones had never looked so defeated before. Not when his wife left him nor when his dog ran away did he even seem to shed a tear. However, his daughter was dead and everything seemed to hit him at once. Stu was trying to console him but he looked to be transfixed on the ocean. He was a brooding man who clearly wanted revenge.

By the time the ambulances arrived, Emma seemed to be coming out of the shock she suffered. She had been so close to saving Mimi. The sight that greeted her instead would make anyone lose their mind. She got up and walked over to Oliver. She gently placed her hand on his shoulder. He didn't shrug her off like she half expected him to. Instead, he just sat there, staring at the water.

Sheriff Eugene Winslow began to debrief the few deputies he had on patrol. The paramedics made their way over to Tommy and Craig who looked paralyzed with fear. After the initial shock wore off, their parents arrived and they were all sent home.

Emma was getting fed up with it all. She pulled out her cellphone and dialed. Her father picked up on the other end almost immediately. He didn't give her the chance to talk. "This is what happens when you don't listen, Emma dear."

"What are you talking about, Dad?"

"If you left the beaches open, I could have had twenty more patrol boats out there guarding the civilians. However, you chose to lower the chances by closing the beaches of threat and therefore I couldn't send anyone out."

"Oh that's a bald-faced lie and you know it!"

There was silence on the other end.

Emma continued. "Send me reinforcements now. We need them to stop this crocodile!"

"Negative, use what you have," Gregory Darwin said and then hung up the phone.

"Every fucking time!" Emma screamed.

"What?" Tanner asked. He was standing behind her.

"It's nothing. We're on our own."

"Bull, can't we call in the Coast Guard or even the military?"

"We could try but my father would probably tell them to stay at the base and that the problem has been eradicated," Emma explained.

"What kind of power does your dad have?" Tanner asked.

"Too much," Emma said coldly and then walked up the dunes to the stairs and back to her limousine.

The sheriff was there waiting for her.

"What the hell is going on, Emma?" he asked

There was no reason to refrain from it anymore. Emma had no one to turn to for help. The crocodile was out of control and she may have the answer why. She looked to the sheriff and then to Tanner who had walked up beside her.

She had to work with what she had.

"There have been rumors of Darwin Institute dumping chemicals into the everglades. Barrels of toxic waste, etcetera. I didn't buy that for a second. My father is a brilliant man who specializes in growth; namely the animal kind. He can produce cows that can double in size. The same goes for chickens and pigs. However, again, I didn't suspect he was dumping anything. That is until I saw the results."

"The crocodile…" Tanner stated.

"And those huge eggs you saw are probably her offspring," Emma explained.

"Why didn't you warn us?" Tanner asked.

"I didn't think the rumors were true. I didn't want to," Emma said as she grew teary-eyed.

Tanner was going to say something but held back. Sheriff Eugene Winslow stepped in. "So you're telling me that a forty-foot croc is the result of some toxic chemicals in the everglades. Fine, I'll buy that. However, I don't understand why it's just the crocodile and not all the other wildlife? What's next, giant mutant mosquitoes?"

"I really don't know," Emma continued. "However, I do know that the rumors are true. They just have to be. My dad turned against me. He's been planning this ever since I got in office. He would rather have my sister in my place."

"That's all well and good but what are we going to do about Mrs. Croc out there?" Tanner asked.

"We'll find her, kill her, and stuff her for some museum. We just need the right weapon," Sheriff Eugene Winslow said.

"Blowing her up would work but it'd also damage the ecosystem," Tanner replied.

"One stick of dynamite wouldn't hurt and it'd probably do the job," Sheriff Eugene Winslow said.

"That's considering you can get her with just one," Emma's head was spinning. "This is crazy. There has to be another way."

"I'm all ears if you've got another idea," Sheriff Eugene Winslow said.

No one spoke up.

The tide lapped on the shore. Its gentle whooshing sound had its usual calming effect. No one paid it any mind though. Instead, Emma, Tanner, and Sheriff Eugene Winslow were focused on Glen and Vince who were driving further and further out to sea. Their vessel was shrinking on the horizon where the sun began to dip.

***

Ian Lang had always had a crush on his best friend. Even in this day and age, with all this acceptance, he still felt it was wrong though. There were times he still preferred women to men but he'd constantly been trying to fight off the latter attraction. Eventually, he would have to tell his girlfriend that he was bisexual and had a crush on Jude.

The mind games continued when Jude asked him to go scuba diving tonight. His big smile and nicely trimmed hair made Ian's heart flutter and he took him up on his offer. It wasn't enough that he'd be spending the day with him. However, now he could delay when he'd tell Gretchen about his feelings. The longer he stalled the better.

Both men arrived at a remote spot in the middle of the ocean as the sun hugged the horizon and they began to don their scuba gear. Jude was quick to undress. He was now down to his boxers and Ian couldn't help but stare. Jude didn't seem to notice. Either that or he did notice but didn't mind.

Ian was having trouble pulling the suit over his shoulders by the time Jude had been fully decked out in the proper attire for their little adventure. Jude walked behind Ian and pulled the wetsuit over his shoulder blades. He then patted him on the back.

"All set?" Jude asked as he made his way over to the port side.

"You bet!" Ian said after the initial shock wore off.

That had been the closest Jude had been to him yet. With that memory tucked nicely in the back of his mind, Ian walked over and sat next to him.

"Let's do this, bro!" Jude said, giving him a fist pump.

The two then dived over the side and into the water. While the surface had been a darker shade of blue, underwater was crystal clear. It was like a utopia for fish of all kinds. Equality was evident to Ian. No fish were discriminated against like Jude had been. Him being a Mexican played a part in Ian's attraction to him.

Soon, they were a few meters down. The bottom was no more than ten. It wasn't the deepest part of the Floridian waters off this particular coast but it was one known for its expansive view. Ian could see miles out but they might as well have been a few hundred because it was all blue. However, when he looked down, that all changed. It was like looking at the world's largest fish tank.

Five meters down and Ian's skin crawled as he saw a big grouper swallow some poor colorful fish. At first he wanted to cry but then realized that this world was much different than the one above. It wasn't about what color the fish were. Instead, it was survival of the fittest. Ian began to not like it down there.

Soon, they touched the bottom. Jude grabbed out his phone and took a photo. It was crazy to think how far technology had gone. Your phone could go underwater with you and still work. Ian struck a pose where he put his hand on his hip and picked his chin up in a fashionable pose.

Jude took the photo despite how gay it literally looked. He liked Ian well and good enough but he just wasn't his type. Too pale and fragile, Ian was a softy. Jude needed a muscular brute in his life. One with olive skin and maybe a porn moustache.

He raised his phone again to take another picture when he saw something swimming in the blue haze behind Ian. His hands shot down and he dropped his expensive cellular device. Ian went to swim to him but Jude kicked away and began to swim to the surface. He was going too fast. Ian was about to scream that he'd get the bends if he didn't slow down but somehow forgot he was underwater.

Then another thought came about.

Why is he doing this? Is there something wrong? Did he see something? Ian spun around and saw nothing. All of a sudden, the area became dark with shade. He looked up and saw that the shadow was there because of a giant reptile. Its white scaly belly shifted with muscle movement as it made its way upwards.

Jude began to feel cramps and his nose was bleeding profusely. Decompression sickness came over him and his world turned into a whirlwind of bubbles and blood. Then, he felt a tight pain in his foot. He managed to force his head to look down. The crocodile had him and was pulling him back down.

All the pressure that built up in Jude's head suddenly hit him like a punch to his face. He was barely conscious when the crocodile began to shake him to and fro. His insides turned to jelly and then fell out when the skin ripped. He was deflated by the time the crocodile began to swallow.

Ian watched in horror as his best friend and possible lover was torn apart right in front of his eyes. He decided right then and there to swim away. While peeling out of there he realized that Jude had left him to save himself. The coward didn't care for him at all in the long run. He had to save himself now.

Anger brewed within Ian as he charged for a nearby rock formation. There was a little tunnel that was see-through at first glance. It'd have to do. He placed himself carefully on a flat rock. The coral scratched him, giving him the ultimate butt itch. He shot up and hollered inside his mask. He rose and rose and suddenly, the crocodile came from behind above a rock formation. With one quick yank, Ian's head was separated from the rest of his body which sank limply to the bottom of the ocean floor. It lay there ten meters down.

***

Glen and Vince had arrived at the scene too late. They had seen the charter boat when the sun had begun to set. By the time they got there, the sun was just barely over the horizon.

"Looks like they went for a love dive," Glen said.

Vince focused the beam coming from the spotlight on the water next to the vessel. It was churning red. He didn't think anyone was alive down there. There was no way with that much blood. Finally, he shut the spotlight off.

"Ain't we supposed to be hunting?" Glen asked.

"Yeah."

"Then turn the spotlight back on, damnit!"

Vince didn't budge. "You just don't understand."

"What's there not to understand, Warner?" Glen asked.

"We can't just kill this crocodile. It's too valuable. Too important." Vince looked down at himself.

"I feckin' knew it!" Glen shouted.

"Keep it down, she might hear you." Vince was shushing him with his hand gestures.

"No, this has gone too far. I've seen some weird shit in the everglades lately. Critters bigger than normal."

"I don't want that crocodile destroyed!" Vince shouted all of a sudden.

There was a brief silence between the two of them.

"Start the boat. We're getting out of here," Glen said.

Vince didn't waste any time. With great haste he maneuvered to the control board and pushed the throttle. The boat began to make good speed. They were out of any danger as far as they knew.

"Thank you for understanding, Mr. Porter."

"Mhm." Glen was grouchy and Vince couldn't figure out why.

***

'Night had taken over. The star-covered sky was hazy with the heat of the ocean rising. It was a particularly muggy night. It was a fact driven home by Sheriff Eugene Winslow constantly taking out a rag and wiping his forehead and neck.

He, Emma, and Tanner watched as Glen and Vince returned from their short hunt. The two had figured that there was no use trying to find the croc tonight. The humidity would cover the quick glimpses they would've had before the reptile sank below.

Mitch and Lola were by Stu. Oliver sat over near the pier. He wanted to be left alone, understandably so. Everyone kept to themselves for the most part.

As the boat drifted into the slip, Glen hopped out and trudged up the stairs and straight for Emma.

"What the hell is going on here?!" he practically screamed.

"The crocodile is a result of my father's work," Emma stated.

"No shit. Color me surprised," Glen was annoyed. He felt like he was the only one to be putting the pieces together. "And you thought if you paid off fish and game that there'd be no complications?"

"I had nothing to do with this!" Emma shouted.

Tanner gently took her by her arm. "It's not worth it, Emma."

"Oh, so now this turd is on a first name basis with ya?" Glen's face turned red.

"What are you getting at, man?" Tanner asked sternly.

"We were supposed to be getting rid of these kids, Mayor. Not promote what they're doing."

"What exactly do you think we're going to do?"

"Oh, ya know. Mess with our traps, tamper with our bait, sip lattes with the foam on top while you criticize everyone you think is wrong without any amount of substantial evidence to support your complaints. Hipster shit basically."

"That's it." Tanner was fuming now. "I'm so sick of people calling us what we're not. We're not activists, we're barely conservationists. We just try to see what changes are happening to the environment. Hell, the only things we do with animals is tag them! You're just the kind of person who likes to lump every group into one category. I'm more conservative than you might realize, Mr. Porter!"

"Is that so?" Glen chuckled. He had to hand it to the kid. Most people he chastised would've whined and complained and screamed by now.

"Gentlemen, please! We can discuss politics at a later date. We need to focus on the plan," Emma said.

Tanner and Glen remained staring, eyes fixed on each other's.

"Okay, kid. We're gonna get this croc and then we'll figure you out." Glen grinned sinisterly.

"No need. I already told you how I roll. Maybe you should spend more time figuring yourself out," Tanner said and then walked away.

Sheriff Eugene Winslow looked over at Glen and then to Vince. The two had obviously had some words between themselves when they were out on the water.

"Mr. Warner, I assume I'll have a full report about what's going on out there and what that animal is by the morning."

"I don't owe you squat," Vince snarled.

"I think you do if you want to keep working these everglades," Emma said.

She then followed Tanner to the van. "Was there anything in the swamp you or your group came across that wasn't part of it?" Emma asked.

"What do you mean?" Tanner questioned her with a look of bewilderment.

"You know, like toxic waste or anything that was dumped there."

"Our findings came up clean. However, we didn't search around the bend much. There could've been something. Her nest is there near the atoll so it's safe to say that, if there was something she was feeding on, she'd want to stick close to it."

"Well then, we need to go out there and stop her in her own territory."

"There's a problem with that plan," Tanner said.

"What?"

"She's not there right now. She's in the ocean and we have no idea when she'll be back."

Sheriff Eugene Winslow approached. "That gives us all the more time to head out there and properly arm the area with explosives and await her return."

"We'll need three groups. One to maintain the beaches, one to hunt down mama croc, and one to make sure that the nest is ready," Tanner explained.

Stan and Oliver approached the group, followed closely by Vince and Glen.

"We'll hunt down the beast," Oliver said coldly.

"Oliver, why don't you go home and get some rest," Emma said sympathetically.

"I appreciate that, Mayor. However, I will not be able to rest until that animal is dead."

There was silence.

"Alright," Sheriff Eugene Winslow began. "Oliver, Stan, Vince, and I will patrol the waters. Mitch, Lola, you both are now deputized along with these hunters. I need you to make sure the beaches stay empty. Glen, Tanner . . . you both head back to the atoll and set the charges. Hopefully we can drive the crocodile to you."

"What about me?" Emma asked.

Secretly, Sheriff Eugene Winslow wished she just went home. She was becoming too concerned and motherly to take the situation seriously. Or so he felt. "You go with Mitch and Lola."

"Why?"

"Because it'd be a good idea to have an authority figure there to back up their claims of the water not being safe."

Thankfully, Emma didn't object.

The sheriff tossed Vince some keys. "Go to the evidence locker at the station. There's some dynamite we snagged from a couple who thought it was a good idea to go fishing with it."

Glen had a sudden flashback to him and Richie Stillwell doing the exact same thing but with more dire consequences. The crocodile attacked and killed Richie. That seemed like forever ago now.

"Alright, let's get to it," Sheriff Eugene Winslow said.

The three groups departed.

CHAPTER FIFTEEN

Her adrenaline increased.

The combination of the speed, the passing water, and the breeze in her hair made it seem like Claire Miller was on top of the world. Having a great, wealthy life here in Florida was more than anyone could ask for. The area she and her husband resided in was full of luxury for the higher class. Tony was particularly enthusiastic and made for fun nights at parties and even at home. He was a ball of energy.

Add on top of that the accelerating and exhilarating water skiing and she felt in total control of her life – complete domination.

As the speedboat drove with her attached by a line with a handlebar and a pair of skis, it covered a great distance in a short amount of time. The husband and wife pair started at the docks at their estate and were now several miles down the shoreline from it. It seemed as though Tony was increasing speed after every few hundred feet.

Claire was just happy to be out on the water. Last night was a fun event with Tony getting plastered and then having his way with her ferociously. However, now looking down into the crystal clear water off a beach not far from her home, she began to appreciate its natural beauty.

Occasionally looking back, Tony often focused on the view ahead. He was testing his new speedboat out to see if it'd live up to the name. He wasn't sure if his wife could tell that every five-hundred feet he'd go an extra two miles per hour but that was beside the point. When he did look over his shoulder, he could see she was having a great time. It was just an added bonus that she was wearing his favorite bikini of hers. It was yellow with pink flowers on the bottom of both corners. He could see her dirty blonde hair whipping around and the water splashing against her tanned body, creating a shine to her.

She was gorgeous despite being a typical snooty, pompous upper class California native. The suggestion to move to Florida with him took some convincing. Regardless, everything fell into place smoothly. Now, with his two million dollar summer condo in the rear view, he could actually focus on her and not stuff that could be done at the house.

They were a rare rich couple in some ways. Both loved each other beyond the money factor. Claire had always been wealthy but Tony wasn't so lucky. The two met at a convention when Tony had been trying to push a product called *The Seed Picker 2000*. It was designed to take the seeds out of watermelons and be compactable enough to store in one's kitchen. Even as he explained it to Claire's father that it basically sifted through the fruit and took the seeds out by a thin straw, Claire couldn't help be enamored by him. He spoke with a strong confidence and was easy on the eyes.

Her father bought the invention and it took off for a bit. It was the number one summer seller of 2019 under the new name *The Seed Sifter*. Claire often joked that it could've been called the seed sniffer. Tony thought it was funny.

Now, on the water, his eyes themselves were sifting through the waves as he looked for rocks. They were coming up on a shallow coral bed and he was attempting to take a left turn in a graceful manner.

Claire rode her skis in a half-circle as he performed the maneuver. She cheered him on with a few fist pumps into the air. Tony looked back and saw a rock formation right behind Claire. He was thankful that it was just a close call.

As he drove on, he looked down next to his seat and opened up a cooler. Inside were some waters. He wasn't about to lose his boating license by drinking alcohol. He grabbed a bottle and tilted his head back with it pressed to his lips. Nothing came out. He then realized he hadn't taken the cap off. He let go of the steering wheel and quickly undid it. As he took another attempted swig, he looked over his shoulder. Claire was still smiling and she gave him a wave. However, something was amiss.

That rock formation was still behind her.

He took his free hands and shielded his eyes from the sun's rays. Squinting, he turned further around and, in doing so, pressed a bit harder on the pedal.

"What in the world?"

It was still hard to make out but it appeared to be moving behind Claire – closing the gap quick. Suddenly, he noticed that Claire was pointing at him, screaming.

She continued shouting and pointing ahead of him. The look of horror on her face told him that something was seriously wrong. However, half his attention was dedicated to trying to figure out what was coming up from behind Claire.

Finally, after ripping his gaze away from the rock formation, he finally understood what she was doing. She was pointing ahead of him. There was something else in the water and he was about to run into it.

He quickly turned around and saw the rather large hull of a yacht. Before he could even put one hand back on the steering wheel, the bow of his speedboat collided into it. Fiberglass shattered as the whole framework got smashed in. The pilot seat quickly connected with the broken pieces of wood and engulfed Tony. The engine followed soon after.

In her shock, Claire managed to wonder why her husband was so focused on her and not what was ahead of him. That was all cut short though when the explosion occurred. The line that held her began to slacken just as the flames engulfed her too.

The crocodile didn't seem fazed by the eruption or the ball of fire, not even as it covered her head and back. She managed to pull her nictitating lens over her eyes and dunk her head slightly under the water before the flames reached her.

She still sensed the human aroma but now it was stronger with a mixture of blood. The coppery smell was a bit different though – hotter. Still, the crocodile swam towards her prey and chomped down on it. It was searing in heat. However, the crocodile began to swallow her prize and swim downward to cooler waters. It had the desired effect of making her food more edible and less unbearably hot.

Suddenly, she sensed something more. It was back on the surface. Right above where she now resided. It was a whooshing sound, as if water was being sucked into an empty bucket. She then heard the splashing about. There was more prey up there now.

Misty Ford had planned this trip with her new boyfriend for a year now. After divorcing her husband and getting a hefty settlement after the court ruled in her favor, she bought a yacht. It came with all the newest gadgets and designs. She laughed when he first went into the cabin below. There was a saltwater fish tank filled with piranha. They reminded her of her money-grubbing husband.

The man was the owner of several businesses and even a producer on a few major motion pictures. She remembered hearing about one of them involving a weird cat/lizard thing and that it attacked some park. She scoffed at his investment.

As time went on and the romance part of their relationship began to dwindle, she resorted to cheating on him with the boyfriend she sat with sun tanning on her yacht at that very moment. The man was a total slime but was good in bed. He portrayed Ian's lover. It was no shock to her that Ian was a homosexual. The last she had heard from him he was actually in Florida with some Hispanic scuba instructor.

Gerald, her acting coach and new boyfriend, put on a marvelous performance. He claimed that he was involved with Ian's affair and even went into great detail about their 'love'. Misty gave him incriminating evidence and the case was won.

"Would you like something to drink, babe?" Gerald asked her as she peeled her eyes open. She hadn't realized she was so close to falling asleep.

"Sure! Margarita with sugar on the rim."

"Of course!" Gerald chuckled and walked below.

There was a humming sound. She looked up and saw a water skier being pulled by a speedboat.

She smiled and lay back down. She wanted to relax some more before having to head back into town. Her mind drifted and she thought about how much fun it would be to have another woman around. She knew Gerald would like that and she knew just the right ones that'd tickle his fancy. She could go either way when she was in the right mood.

Brmmmmmmmm.

Thinking back to last night, she remembered their little experiment in bed. Gerald went to town on her for a minute straight. Thrusting faster and faster and yet he showed no signs of finishing any time soon. She believed he could last for forty-five minutes given the time of day. He did his best when he was on the cusp of being tired.

Faster and faster, he gave her an orgasm that just kept building. The sheets were shifting around as their shiny bodies worked their magic. It all built and built until...

Boom!

Misty snapped out of it and shot up. Smoke began to rise and she could smell gasoline spilling into the ocean. Then the orange flames came.

"Gerald!"

She ran to the cabin door and saw that he was leaning against the guardrail on the staircase.

"What the hell happened?!" Gerald said in-between wheezy coughs.

"I don't know but I think someone hit us!"

His coughing fit worsened as they walked to the side of the boat. The smoke was almost unbearable now. She could not even see the boat through it all.

Suddenly, she pinpointed where it was when a massive explosion occurred, sending her and Gerald flying back and over the guardrail.

Splash.

Gerald surfaced first and swam over towards Misty. She was unconscious. "Babe! Babe, wake up!"

He grabbed her by the arm and turned her over. Half her face was burnt away along with hair and half her ear. Her eyeball dangled from its socket.

"Oh my god!"

He shot backwards and backstroked a few feet before the reality sunk in. She was dead. He swam back a bit further until he bumped into something. It felt rough like a rock. However, they weren't that far in. . . were they?

Gerald turned around and saw it staring at him. Its head and jaws were above the surface while the rest was submerged. Though, judging by the size of the head, the animal was massive.

The only thing that popped into his mind was to act this out. He decided to play possum.

Gripping his chest, he faked a heart-attack and began to float on his back. He hoped to God that the animal bought it. It had been thirty seconds or so when he looked down. It was still there. However, now, it was opening its mouth. The cavernous jaws spread wide. The lower jaw lifted him on top of its jagged yellow teeth.

Gerald reeled over and tried to climb out as the upper jaw slowly came down. It was hard but he managed to slip through the teeth without puncturing his body. He felt himself falling. Then the searing pain began.

He was still falling but now with one less limb. His leg had been detached by a bite from the crocodile's jaws. He plummeted into the ocean, the saltwater stinging his exposed flesh. He grabbed his stump and screamed.

Just then, the area around him grew lighter. The crocodile was swimming away. Gerald tried to compose himself and surfaced carefully without much movement. He then bobbed there for a few seconds and then he saw a long, scaly appendage slam down towards him.

The crocodile's tail crushed his skull and sent his head into his shoulders.

***

Emma Darwin was just getting on the beach when Mitch and Lola began screaming for people to get out of the water. At first, everyone looked at them in a funny, head-tilting manner. Kids began to splash in their general direction and some even went as far as to flip them off.

Lola scoffed at a particularly annoying brat who began kicking up sand on her. She was about to grab the kid and do god knows what when Emma approached her and tried to calm her down. "These people need our help." "Yeah, well they have a funny way of showing their gratitude," she shot back with her thick Australian accent.

Meanwhile, Mitch was ushering people out of the water. Some people listened while others approached him. One of them pulled down his khaki shorts revealing his privates. Lola got a glimpse before he covered them with his hands. She was impressed but quickly returned her attention to the matters at hand.

Emma approached the lifeguard stand and demanded that everyone be told to get out of the water. The man in question didn't seem too phased. He was probably young, younger than Tanner even. She wondered if he even knew who she was.

"Damnit, kid! Get the megaphone out and call everyone in! It's coming!"

"What's coming?"

As if to answer his reply, a sudden explosion grabbed everyone's attention.

"She's   here!"

The young lifeguard began to corral everyone in with his amplified voice through the megaphone. Some were reluctant but eventually everyone started to come in.

"Mommy, look! It's an alligator!"

Emma, Lola, and Mitch turned just in time to see the tail smash down on a man. Then their heads followed that tail all the way up the scaly hide of the crocodile. Soon, they focused on the black head and yellow eyes as a cavernous mouth opened and a booming roar exploded from the animal. It held for ten seconds and then the crocodile ducked under the water.

"Everyone, hurry!" Mitch screamed.

Just then, rapid gunfire was heard. Emma turned to see the sheriff unloading on the monster. The bullets rang true but did little to affect her. The crocodile's body slithered along the surface like a snake and approached the bathers.

As the shots continued, Mitch saw an old man wheezing and trying to make it to shore. The crocodile was a mere fifty yards from him and closing fast. He trudged out and tried to make it to him before he could be engulfed in those hideous jaws.

Sheriff Eugene Winslow began to scream as his M-16 shot every round until the clip ran out. He moved over and let Vince take his place. He aimed his trusty bolt-action rifle, fired, and then reloaded it, which dispensed of the fired cartridge. The action was repeated several times until his gun ran dry as well. Then it was Stan's turn. They were coming up on the crocodile and he brought out his pump-action shotgun. He got off one shot and then cocked it. However, before the shell even hit the ground from the last shot, their boat lifted out of the water. Oliver looked around and noticed that it was not the female croc's doing.

This seemed to get the attention of their target which turned and looked at them. It was almost as if she were in awe. The boat began to rise higher and higher and then slid backwards. The four men fell and slipped about.

"What the hell is going on?!" Vince screamed.

"Shouldn't you have all the answers?" Sheriff Eugene Winslow snapped back.

The boat then began to fall upside down and, from beneath, a scaly head emerged. Stan turned and began to raise his shotgun at the second crocodile when he lost his balance and slipped off the port side.

On shore everyone was screaming uncontrollably and running about.

The female crocodile changed direction and came towards her long lost sibling. The male shook off the battered boat and let it land upturned into the ocean.

Stan was the first to surface and see that the crocodiles were nipping at each other. It was as if they hadn't seen each other in years. He then turned and saw Oliver.

"Ollie, man! Let's get the hell to shore!"

"What about the sheriff and the game warden?!"

"They'd better keep up!" Stan said and began to make a break for the shallows.

Oliver was about to follow suit when he saw that the crocodiles had turned their attention to Stan. He stopped dead in the water. He felt small yet insignificant to the larger than life reptiles. Stan had no idea what was coming and Oliver wanted to scream for his friend to stop. However, that'd put him in harm's way and he had to avenge his daughter.

All he could do was watch, wait, and pray.

Stan continued onward, unaware of the two pairs of glowing yellow eyes following him. Just then, Vince Warner burst from the depths in front of him. He gasped for breath but Stan pushed him out of the way. He never liked the prick anyway.

However, he did tolerate Oliver. He turned back to see if his friend was following him but, instead he saw the two crocodiles grab Vince and begin to fight over him like two dogs would a chew toy. However, their tug-of-war ended much quicker with Vince ripping in two after the sounds of bones splintering followed by innards spilling into the ocean.

What dawned on Stan right then wasn't that the man before him was dead. It was how close the crocodiles were to him. He reached for a hunting knife he decided to carry and figured it was the least he could do to defend himself. The crocodiles charged and Stan lunged for them. They dwarfed him in every way but he still went down fighting. It wasn't much of a battle. The crocodile's mouth encompassed him and closed down on his entire body save for his forearm. He dropped the knife and was swallowed whole by the female.

Oliver prayed they'd leave. He just didn't want them to attack anyone anymore. Just then, Sheriff Eugene Winslow emerged from the deep and quickly grabbed a piece of splintered wood. Out of the four men who were attacked, he was the most banged up from the initial blow. He could barely even see straight. Oliver doggy-paddled over towards the lawman but realized that the two crocodiles, swimming side by side, were going to pass right by him.

"Sheriff, remain still. Don't make a sound," Oliver whispered hoarsely.

It was as if Sheriff Eugene Winslow couldn't hear him or couldn't help it. He coughed once as the crocodiles swam past and then he was gone, sucked under the waves leaving behind a blood trail as they dragged him further away.

Emma was on her knees crying as Lola brought Mitch and the old guy in. She couldn't believe it. The one man who stood up for her was gone. It was then she realized that she never gave him the recognition he deserved.

The lifeguard approached Mitch and Lola and took over helping the old man. "Hey, man. Do you have a radio we can borrow?"

With his free hand, the young lifeguard handed him his two-way. "I'll need that back."

"Don't worry," Mitch said.

Emma watched as the crocodiles went further out. They were heading in the direction of the everglades.

CHAPTER SIXTEEN

It was too quiet.

Glen Porter eased the boat onto the shore of the atoll. As he shut the engine off, Tanner grabbed out a tranq-gun that he had stored in a steel case. Glen wanted to laugh at the kid but realized that this wasn't the time. It was a serious matter that needed to be handled professionally.

He then recalled the time Richie was killed not too far from this area in particular. The swamp was coated in darkness at that time and he didn't see her coming. There was no way to stop the force of nature from claiming his friend's life. This time would be different. He reached into his wooden case and pulled out an assault rifle with armor piercing rounds.

The radio crackled and got both men's attention. Tanner tried to answer it but Glen grabbed him by the shoulder.

"What?!"

He shushed him and then pointed out to the opening of the cove.

She was there, her scaly hide glistening in the evening sun. She submerged and then made it up onto the sandbank that was blanketed in a thick haze. They heard a flapping sound as her webbed feet slushed around and propelled her further inland. They barely heard the quick splash as her tail snaked out of the water, quivering above the surface as it was dragged.

"*T-o — 'em!*" a man's voice came over the radio. It sounded like Mitch.

"What's he saying?" Glen asked.

"I don't know. Will you shut up so I can hear him?" Tanner snapped back.

There was silence on the other end of the radio.

Glen decided to take matters into his own hands. He turned back towards the sandbank and scanned the brush. She was there, he could see her. Even if she thought she was hidden, she was too big. You'd have to put a train in front of her to hide her. Even then, it might not be enough.

He checked over his rifle. The cartridge was in place and the safety was off. He then looked through his scope. The crocodile came into view. He followed her black hide all the way from the tip of her tail to her bright yellow eyes. She seemed to see him yet not see him. That was the thing about reptiles that creeped Glen out. You could never tell what they were thinking or even looking at. It was almost as if there was more going on in that thick skull than he gave them credit for.

"Can you hear me? There's. . ." Mitch's voice cut out again.

"Hang on, I've almost got him," Tanner said as he adjusted the knob.

Never taking his eyes off the crocodile before him, Glen did spare some attention to Tanner. "Tell him to try a different station."

"Try a different station, Mitch," Tanner said immediately as if he had already thought of it before Glen said anything.

The two men waited in silence. The swamp sounds were coming back yet the crocodile didn't move. However, the noises of nature were more like warnings. Glen focused on the crocodile's eyes. His finger pressed against the trigger. Just then, static came through on the radio and Tanner focused on it, pressing the radio to his ear. He didn't see the water swell next to him.

The female then gave it away. She was now looking directly at Glen who felt his blood run cold. It almost appeared as if she were grinning at him.

"There's two!" Mitch's voice screamed over the radio.

Just then, the boat rocketed upward. Glen and Tanner were rising up into the air above it. After seemingly being suspended in animation for a solid minute, the boat landed back onto the muddy shores of the atoll and Glen and Tanner hit the framing hard.

Before Tanner could even sit up, Glen was on his feet and firing at the crocodile on the shore. He managed to shoot that evil eye and two eggs next to her. The crocodile roared in pain and then charged towards the water. Glen fired until his clip ran out and then he ran for his wooden gun case. It wasn't there.

"Shit! The fuckin' thing must've fallen overboard when that second big bastard hit us!" Tanner looked over at Glen who was seething.

"Let's get the hell out of here!" he suggested but then realized the engine was gone as well. It was listing five feet behind them in the swamp. "Oh crap!"

The male crocodile was nowhere in sight.

Glen looked around. No weapons, no defense.

"Alright, here's what we're going to do. I'm going to go get the motor, you keep an eye out for them. If you see any sign of them, shout. Then, when I get back, you help me lug the motor aboard."

"I'll go," Tanner protested

"This has nothing to do with being treated equal or being the hero. You're stronger than me. I need you to lift it aboard. Think you can handle that?"

Glen didn't give Tanner time to answer. He began to make his way over the guardrail and into the water. Entering the lukewarm lagoon, a heaviness seemed to weigh him down. Nearby, there was an old rotted tree that's branches hung low. He figured that if he couldn't get back to Tanner in time, he always had a second option for escape. As he inched closer and closer to the boat motor, he could see the propeller glistening in the sunlight that barely peeked through the trees. The ray of light seemed to act as a guide from the heavens as it shone on it. This made Glen want to hasten his pace. He composed himself and moved closer to the motor and further away from Tanner.

A breezy chill ran down Tanner's back. It must have been ninety degrees out with unbearable humidity. He wondered why he suddenly felt cold. He then took in a sharp breath. He hadn't realized he'd been holding it in. He was going to take another when he saw the water start to move in an unnatural way. . . as if it were rushing past something in a V-shape. With his newly injected air, he shouted hoarsely. "Glen!"

He slowly turned and saw that Tanner was pointing to the water to his right. Besides some lily pads coasting along, the surrounding area was still. However, Glen knew better. That thing had snuck up on him and Richie with ease.

Struggling to make his next move, Glen resorted to slowly submerging beneath the swampy water. He was up to his chest, then his chin, and then he was eye level with the surface. He looked up at Tanner who was frozen in fear. Then, he went under.

"Glen!" Tanner shouted again. "Don't do this to me, man!"

There was no response.

On the placid surface, Tanner could not tell that Glen was absolutely horrified. He was staring face to face with a twenty-eight foot, red-eyed crocodile. This one was smaller than its mate and yet seemed all the more ferocious. The crocodile hovered a few feet from the bottom of the cove. Its legs were protruding out in an awkward position. Glen was mesmerized. It was a few seconds before the reptile's right claw began to slowly move through the water, followed by its left, and then two back claws. Glen, in a similar motion, brought his hand to his belt and slowly pulled out his Bowie knife.

"Glen!" Tanner was freaking out. "Glen! We have to get out of here. Together, man!"

The muffled sounds of Tanner made Glen realize how close he was to help. He barely paid that or even Tanner any mind. Instead, his arms opened and he awaited battle.

"C'mon, old man!" Tanner was furious and scared.

Splash.

Tanner turned to see that the female crocodile, in her forty-foot length, was already nudging the boat with her snout. Her tail wasn't even in the water fully.

"Get away!" he screamed.

There was nowhere to go. No weapons to aid him besides his lousy tranq-gun. He had to do something to survive. If not for him, for Emma. The thought of the red-haired, fair beauty gave him a small amount of courage. It was all he could muster. He looked over and saw the branches of the rotted tree and decided to take his chances.

Tanner hopped off the boat and onto the atoll. He then charged into the dirty cove water. Trudging forward, he didn't dare look back. Not even as the boat he and Glen came in on was toppled over with the crocodile crawling over its hull.

The sound of fiberglass breaking almost got his attention but he continued on, ever forward towards hopeful sanctuary. If he could climb higher and higher up the tree, maybe he'd be safe.

Her scales made a rough, grinding sound as she finally made it over the boat and onto the atoll. Soon, she was in the water and moving considerably faster. This time, Tanner quickly looked over his shoulder and then snapped his head back doing a double take. She was less than a foot away from him. Splashing in the frothing water he was in denial even though he knew what was inevitably coming.

Just then, his back hit something. He felt down in the water and realized he was right next to the tree for there was roots and wood all around. He reached and grabbed a tree limb and thrust it out of the water and in front of him. The crocodile's jaws snapped around the end of it and she began to shake it with him still hanging on. He was lifted into the air and, when he looked up, he saw a low-hanging branch. He let go of the other limb and grabbed onto it. He wanted to cheer and begin to climb when he heard a cracking sound.

The cracking sound amplified into thousands of tiny ones. It sounded like rope twisting. That was when he realized the branch wouldn't support him and his heart sank.

Below, the crocodile tossed the gnarled piece of wood and opened her jaws into the air. As expected, the branch started to bend, lowering Tanner closer and closer into the awaiting cavernous mouth. He held on for dear life as the branch tilted downward and then snapped off the old rotted tree and right into the crocodile's mouth.

However, Tanner didn't feel any searing pain. No teeth could be felt buried in his flesh. He opened his eyes, having not realized he closed them, and saw that he was indeed in the crocodile's mouth. However, the branch was lodged in her throat.

Tanner quickly rolled over and out of the jaws and into the water.

The one-eyed female was soon gagging uncontrollably. Her prey backstroked while looking at her. She became enraged.

Just then, Tanner felt a pair of powerful hands grab him. He looked up and saw it was Glen. He was on another boat. There were a group of hunters behind him. He was covered in blood. Tanner then looked back and saw that the two crocodiles were close together and bleeding.

Glen handed Tanner a rifle and pointed towards the engine. The activist didn't hesitate. He shouldered the weapon and took aim at the boat motor. The crocodiles gurgled in agony. He noticed that Glen had stuck the male in the throat and carved downward.

One shot.

Bang!

The heat of the explosion caused Glen and Tanner and two of the other hunters to fall back.

Singed a bit, Glen sat up, as did Tanner and the others. They all stared at the burning carcasses of the two apex predators of the everglades, now smoldering in the peeking sun.

***

"This is Darwin speaking."

"Dad, the problem has been taken care of," Emma said.

"How so, Em?" her father asked.

"I've just received word that the reptiles have been eliminated."

"Are you sure of this?"

"I trust the people of Graceville, Daddy."

There was a long, drawn out pause.

"I'm proud of you then, Emma," Gregory Darwin said in a way that confused her.

He seemed empathetic yet proud. There wasn't a sense of finality or even relief. Instead of feeling like it was all over, Emma Darwin stood there in silence.

"I have to go now," Gregory said.

Emma snapped out of it. "Okay, I'll keep you updated."

"If you insist."

"What do you mean, 'if I insist'?"

"I mean, if the problem is all over," he paused. "You know what, never mind. Come by tonight for dinner. We have things to discuss. You, me and your sister."

Emma looked up and saw the boat approaching with Tanner standing up tall and proud.

"Can we do that tomorrow night? I have plans already." She smiled and gingerly waved at Tanner.

"I suppose I can take a rain check for just tonight. We'll make it breakfast tomorrow then?"

"I would but I have a speech to prepare and then give to the people."

"Lunch?"

"Lunch."

Emma expected her father to just hang up the phone but to her surprise, he had more to say. "Goodbye."

"Bye, Daddy." She hung up the phone and a sense of relief washed over her.

It was now truly over.

As Tanner stepped onto the docks, Emma rushed to him and planted a kiss on his lips. He fully embraced it. When she pulled away, he noticed she was blushing. "Perhaps we could give us a try."

"I'd love that," Tanner said and they kissed again under the harsh sunlight.

CHAPTER SEVENTEEN

No longer empty.

Emma Darwin rolled on her side. She was wearing a black cocktail dress with a deep, floral V-neck that exposed her massive cleavage. The night prior, Tanner had gawked at her appearance. Her red hair was done up and wavy and she had shiny pink lipstick on her inviting lips. They had ended up kissing and groping each other so much that they were asked to leave the restaurant.

They didn't argue and Emma drove them to her house. There, they were so quick to make love that they didn't undress. Instead, Emma slipped off her black silk panties and opened her legs. He mounted her but in a gentle way. Every so often he would cup her face with his palm, and she'd kiss it.

Once he was ready, he pulled out. There needed to be more sexual interactions. Kids would come later. Tanner knew she wanted children, and he would happily oblige.

The alarm went off and Emma awoke to Tanner looking at her. "You sleep like an angel." He smiled and they kissed.

She got up and gently took his hand. Guiding him to the bath, she turned on the faucet. It poured warm water into the porcelain tub as they climbed in.

Her pink nipples pressed against his hairy chest and he found his way back inside her. They both let out an uncontrollably loud moan and giggled. Shortly after they got out, Emma's publicist knocked on the door and she received the notes for the speech.

"You ready for this?" Tanner asked.

"More than ready." She turned and smiled at him.

***

The crowd cheered as Glen and Tanner stepped onto the stage to sit at the available chairs. Alongside them were Oliver, Mitch, and Lola. The cameras were rolling which did make them a little nervous. However, once Emma walked up to the podium, all sense of worry was lost.

Silence.

It was a peaceful thing.

"The past two weeks have been hard," Emma began. "Especially after one certain day where a pair of rogue crocodiles terrorized our shores and everglades. However, several people helped to stop the menaces and save our homes. They will be rewarded while others, who also contributed, won't be able to accept this token of appreciation. Kyle Felton, Tiffany Baker, Dallas Jacobson, Stanley Jedson, Vince Warner, and even our sheriff, Eugene Winslow amongst many others gave great sacrifice to discover and stop these man-eaters. As far as we know, twenty people had been killed and their lives will never be forgotten."

The crowd remained silent.

"I present this ribbon of honor and respect to Glen Porter, Lola Besser, Mitch Carter, Oliver Jones, and Tanner Felton."

The five of them stood as the crowd erupted into cheers. Reporters started coming closer to the stage. They felt like rock stars. Tanner placed a hand on Emma's shoulder and gave her a kiss on the lips. The town's celebration could be heard for miles.

Suddenly, a helicopter whizzed overhead. It looked like it was trying to land. The swirling blades were so loud that Emma had to cover her ears. She was, however, able to look at the aircraft. It had the words *Darwin Inc.* written on the side. "Daddy?"

She hadn't seen her father in-person in years. She started to make her way towards the edge of the dock. A couple of reporters followed her, as did Tanner.

Out of nowhere, the chopper's side door slid open and someone unloaded at something in the water. There was a huge splash as a reaction to the hailing bullets. Tanner, Emma, and the remaining reporter stood in shock. The other reporter with a whiney voice, glasses and beard ran off the docks and towards his car with a scratch in it. He then recorded the event with his phone from the safety of his vehicle.

"It can't possibly be," Tanner said coldly.

The female crocodile's head rose from the depths a mere fifty yards from the dock. She was still missing an eye, had blood continuously pouring out of her mouth, and was singed on her black scales which was only visible by her yellow underbelly.

"Everyone get back!" Emma screamed.

With a mighty roar, the crocodile's head submerged and began attacking the pilings. Tanner grabbed Emma around the waist just as the wooden planks beneath them began to give way.

Far out across the ocean, the helicopter circled back around for another assault on the reptile.

Meanwhile, Tanner and Emma felt the floor give way. Suddenly, everything came apart. Cracking sounds intensified as the whole end of the dock fell into the surging sea.

Tanner was still on a stable piece while holding onto Emma. She was dangling off the edge.

"No!" Tanner screamed.

"Help me!" Emma screamed in utter horror.

Wet and slippery, he was having trouble staying on top himself let alone being able to lift Emma up. He felt a sense of relief when he heard Mitch, Glen, Lola and Oliver's footsteps running towards him, calling after them.

"Guys, help me!"

The gunner on the chopper took aim just as the female crocodile lunged from the depths and forward towards Emma. The bullets flew at the beast and hit their target. They rode up, starting at her lower back and they'd eventually hit her head.

Emma started to scream wildly as the crocodile drew closer. Its cavernous jaws opened wide. The armor piercing rounds were up to her neck and a roar escaped causing hot air to rush forward. The smell was atrocious and Tanner could barely take it. Still, he held on.

Bullets were raining down right behind the top of her skull where the brain was located.

Click.

The 50CAL jammed and the gunner could only fiddle with it to get the last few rounds into her head.

Tanner watched in horror as the female crocodile bit around Emma's mid-section. Blood erupted from her mouth as her organs turned to jelly.

"No!" Tanner screamed.

Suddenly, the 50CAL roared to life and hit their target. The female crocodile's brain snapped off its stem just as Emma's lower half left her torso. They slid back down into the everglades. Tanner hoisted Emma back up. She looked at him with glazed-over eyes. She was unresponsive. A sad look covered her paling face. Tanner repeated her name over and over again, but she was drifting away. The shock of it all soon silenced them both.

***

It was just an egg.

There was nothing to it. The life form broke from its confines and shell fragments hit the misty earth below. A chirping sound came from within. It was frail like its brother. Finally, spilling onto the ground, the hatchling began to make its way towards the water. However, another part of it wanted to go the other way into the jungle. It pulled and pulled but then it realized it wasn't mental. It was physical.

The two-headed croc had been born.

The End

SEVERED**PRESS**

f facebook.com/severedpress
twitter.com/severedpress

CHECK OUT OTHER GREAT CRYPTID NOVELS

BIGFOOT WAR
by Eric S. Brown

Now a feature film from Origin Releasing. For the first time ever, all three core books of the Bigfoot War series have been collected into a single tome of Sasquatch Apocalypse horror. Remastered and reedited this book chronicles the original war between man and beast from the initial battles in Babblecreek through the apocalypse to the wastelands of a dark future world where Sasquatch reigns supreme and mankind struggles to survive. If you think you've experienced Bigfoot Horror before, think again. Bigfoot War sets the bar for the genre and will leave you praying that you never have to go into the woods again.

CRYPTID ZOO
by Gerry Griffiths

As a child, rare and unusual animals, especially cryptid creatures, always fascinated Carter Wilde.

Now that he's an eccentric billionaire and runs the largest conglomerate of high-tech companies all over the world, he can finally achieve his wildest dream of building the most incredible theme park ever conceived on the planet...CRYPTID ZOO.

Even though there have been apparent problems with the project, Wilde still decides to send some of his marketing employees and their families on a forced vacation to assess the theme park in preparation for Opening Day.

Nick Wells and his family are some of those chosen and are about to embark on what will become the most terror-filled weekend of their lives—praying they survive.

STEP RIGHT UP AND GET YOUR FREE PASS...

TO CRYPTID ZOO

 SEVERED**PRESS**

facebook.com/severedpress
twitter.com/severedpress

CHECK OUT OTHER GREAT CRYPTID NOVELS

SWAMP MONSTER MASSACRE
by **Hunter Shea**

The swamp belongs to them. Humans are only prey. Deep in the overgrown swamps of Florida, where humans rarely dare to enter, lives a race of creatures long thought to be only the stuff of legend. They walk upright but are stronger, taller and more brutal than any man. And when a small boat of tourists, held captive by a fleeing criminal, accidentally kills one of the swamp dwellers' young, the creatures are filled with a terrifyingly human emotion—a merciless lust for vengeance that will paint the trees red with blood.

TERROR MOUNTAIN
by **Gerry Griffiths**

When Marcus Pike inherits his grandfather's farm and moves his family out to the country, he has no idea there's an unholy terror running rampant about the mountainous farming community. Sheriff Avery Anderson has seen the heinous carnage and the mutilated bodies. He's also seen the giant footprints left in the snow—Bigfoot tracks. Meanwhile, Cole Wagner, and his wife, Kate, are prospecting their gold claim farther up the valley, unaware of the impending dangers lurking in the woods as an early winter storm sets in. Soon the snowy countryside will run red with blood on TERROR MOUNTAIN.

SEVEREDPRESS

 facebook.com/severedpress
 twitter.com/severedpress

CHECK OUT OTHER GREAT BIGFOOT NOVELS

THE BEASTS OF STONECLAD MOUNTAIN
by Gerry Griffiths

Clay Morgan is overjoyed when he is offered a place to live in a remote wilderness at the base of a notorious mountain. Locals say there are Bigfoot living high up in the dense mountainous forest. Clay is skeptic at first and thinks it's nothing more than tall tales.

But soon Clay becomes a believer when giant creatures invade his new home and snatch his baby boy, Casey.

Now, Clay and his wife, Mia, must rescue their son with the help of Clay's uncle and his dog, a journey up the foreboding mountain that will take them into an unimaginable world...straight into hell!

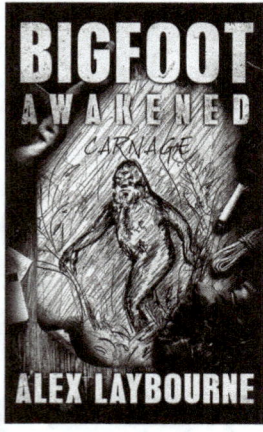

BIGFOOT AWAKENED
by Alex Laybourne

A weekend away with friends was supposed to be fun. One last chance for Jamie to blow off some steam before she leaves for college, but when the group make a wrong turn, fun is the last thing they find.

From the moment they pass through a small rural town they are being hunted by whatever abominations live in the woods.

Yet, as the beasts attack and the truth is revealed, they learn that despite everything, man still remains the most terrifying evil of them all.

www.ingramcontent.com/pod-product-compliance
Lightning Source LLC
Chambersburg PA
CBHW061238170626
46809CB00007B/2735